WRECKED
WITH YOU
J. KENNER
NEW YORK TIMES BESTSELLING AUTHOR

Also By The Author

STARK SECURITY
shattered with you
shadows of you-short story
broken with you
ruined with you

THE STARK SAGA
novels
release me
claim me
complete me
anchor me
lost with me
novellas
take me
have me
play my game
seduce me
unwrap me
deepest kiss
entice me
hold me
please me
indulge me

Praise for J. Kenner's Novels

"*Shattered With You* is a sultry little page turner that comes brimming with scorching passion, edge of your seat action, and heart-wrenching emotion." *Reds Romance Reviews*

"J. Kenner is an exceptional storyteller. The drama, tension, and heat were perfect." *About That Story*

"PERFECT for fans of *Fifty Shades of Grey* and *Bared to You*. *Release Me* is a powerful and erotic romance novel." *Reading, Eating & Dreaming Blog*

"I will admit, I am in the 'I loved *Fifty Shades*' camp, but after reading *Release Me*, Mr. Grey only scratches the surface compared to Damien Stark." *Cocktails and Books Blog*

"It is not often when a book is so amazingly well-written that I find it hard to even begin to accurately describe it . . . " *Romancebookworm's Reviews*

WRECKED
WITH YOU
J. KENNER

NEW YORK TIMES BESTSELLING AUTHOR

M&O

Wrecked With You Copyright © 2020 by Julie Kenner

My Fallen Saint (excerpt) © 2020 by Julie Kenner

Cover design by Michele Catalano, Catalano Creative

Cover image by Annie Ray/Passion Pages

ISBN: 978-1-949925-54-8

Published by Martini & Olive Books

V-2020-5-28P

PROLOGUE

The world is a fucked up place.

That was probably the first lesson I learned in life. A hard-taught lesson when he'd yell at me or slap me. Or worse.

He was supposed to love us. To protect us.

But "supposed to" is only the truth in a fairy tale world. We lived in the real world, my sister and me. And when it got to be too much—when there was nothing and no one we could turn to except each other—that's when we ran.

I've done things I'm ashamed of. Things I had to in order to survive. To keep us safe.

And I learned a long time ago not to trust anyone but myself and my sister. Because the people who are supposed to protect you will fail *you. And the people who are supposed to love you can just as easily be monsters.*

But lately, things have started to shift. My world is opening, and people are surprising me. I'm letting down my guard; I'm letting people in.

It's a mistake, and I know it. Because now he's come into my life.

And though I know I need to keep my distance—though I know damn well that he's going to hurt my heart—I can't help but slide down that hill toward him, terrified all the while that he won't be strong enough to catch me.

And even more scared that he will.

CHAPTER ONE

"Any luck?" Antonio Santos stood with his arms crossed as he stared over Noah's shoulder at the nonsensical string of numbers, letters, and symbols that flowed across the screen in time with the tapping of Noah's fingers on the keys.

"Almost there," Noah said, his attention never veering from the monitor.

Tony shifted his weight, then took a step back and leaned against the massive oak table that made up one of the three sides of Noah's cluttered workspace. Despite being the top dog at the Austin division of Stark Applied Technology, Noah's office looked more like the basement of a kid who loved to code and play video games.

Then again, Tony could hardly fault his

friend for that. Noah Carter had mad skills with computers, electronics, anything tech. Tony had skills, too, but his leaned toward the more deadly variety. A skillset for which he'd been well-paid in the past, though only for jobs that were on the right side of his conscience.

Those paid gigs, though, had been simply a means to an end. Even the time that Tony had spent working with Noah for a vigilante group called Deliverance had been for a purpose. Tony fully supported the work that the group had done rescuing kidnapping victims and taking down their tormentors. But he'd also utilized the organization's massive resources for his own purpose.

Specifically, the search for one man, known only as The Serpent.

Tony could never get back what The Serpent had stolen from him. His mother. His uncle. His whole goddamn life. But he could have revenge.

And he was getting pretty damn close to the prize.

He had Noah to thank for much of his recent progress. His friend was the one who had set Tony up with a secret identity on a notorious dark web message board. A place where, over the span of years, Tony had cultivated a reputation as a badass mercenary with skills for hire. Not a lie ... but not exactly the truth, either.

He'd posted fake details to boost his reputation and taken just enough real jobs to support the cover. But only jobs that he'd vetted first, carefully making sure the targets weren't innocent. In fact, far from it. Murderers, sexual predators, and the like.

He'd built his reputation slowly until he had enough cred to ask questions about The Serpent without attracting too much unwanted attention.

Still, progress had been a slog. For over three months, he received no leads. Then a few trickled in, but none panned out.

Months passed, and even though he'd known that this was a long-haul game, he'd started to lose hope.

Then a private message from The-Asst had appeared. A woman, or so she said. And she promised Tony that although she didn't know where The Serpent was at the moment, she knew how to learn his true identity.

More important, she promised to share that information if Tony would meet her at the exclusive Debauchery Resort, a no-holds-barred sex party island located in the Caribbean.

She named the date—exactly five days from

now—and that was an appointment he intended to keep. So long as it wasn't a trap.

Like his own dark web identity, The-Asst's profile had no identifying information. Which meant that he had no way of verifying if she was even really a woman, much less someone in a position to, possibly, have access to information about The Serpent.

And that, of course, was why Tony had come to Austin to see Noah. Because if anyone could peel through the layers to discover who The-Asst was, it was his tech genius friend.

Dragging his fingers through his close-cropped hair, he once again came up behind Noah as words and symbols flashed rapid-fire across the screen. "What's—"

His friend held up a hand, cutting off Tony's question. "Almost done. Just one more—*yes*. Got it, you slippery little fuck."

Tony looked from the nonsense on the screen to Noah, then back to the screen. There was a reason Tony didn't do tech. There wasn't a damn thing on the screen of interest that he could see.

"I could explain it," Noah said dryly, looking over his shoulder at Tony. "But then I'd have to kill you."

"Funny man." Tony pulled over one of the

chairs and sat, rolling close for a better view of the nonsense. "Don't explain. Just tell me what you've learned."

"I can't get a name for you. Not yet. But I'm working on software that will—"

"—do something magical with bits and bytes and quantum physics. Yeah, man, the whole world knows you're a genius. What's the bottom line?"

"Eighty-seven percent probability your contact really is a woman. I derived that from—"

"Ah, ah. Do I bore you with ballistics?"

Noah rolled his eyes. "There's nothing boring about ballistics, and I'm a damn good shot, too."

"I'm better." Tony grinned, enjoying himself. Hell, the first time he'd laughed in months was last night at Noah and Kiki's new house overlooking Lake Travis.

"Right now, the only cojones that count are mine. You want the intel or not?"

"You know I do." He leaned back in the chair and kicked his feet out, prepared to get schooled.

Surprisingly, though, Noah skipped over the miracles of semiconductors and whatever programming language was in vogue these days. He dove straight to the results from his still-in-beta software.

"I can't confirm your contact is a woman, but the probability is high. And based on where I'm pinging back from the shadow on her messages, she's located in Southern California."

"I didn't think you could trace that kind of thing on the dark web."

"Most can't. I can. At least to a seventy-two percent certainty rate. Like I said, this is still in development."

"So there's a good chance she's in California."

"Either that, or knows her way around this nerdy tech stuff as well as I do and is purposefully shielding not just her location but the shadow of her location that I'm tracking."

"I'm impressed."

Noah grinned, but continued. "Since your intel suggests The Serpent's based around LA, the probability that her information is legit increases."

"All of which means it's worth a shot to meet this woman."

"Sounds to me like she's the best lead you've had."

"Lately, she's been the only lead." He'd had a bead on The Serpent years ago, but the plan had gone horribly wrong, and Tony had lost a hell of a lot more than the year of tracking and planning.

"Women are allowed to arrive alone at Debauchery," Noah continued, and Tony nodded. That much he knew. "Men aren't."

"And she's planning on meeting me there," Tony said. "Yeah, I've thought about it. That means that she assumes I'll find someone to come with me. And it means that she isn't trying to entice me to travel with her. She's probably going early to protect herself or to set a trap."

"Right now, the probabilities are pretty much equal. But I did find a few single seats booked on Debauchery's private jets booked the day before you're set to meet her."

"Any names?"

"Nope. Their security is tight. Not surprising considering the nature of the resort. I'm sure I can get around it if you think it's important. Want me to keep poking?"

Tony shook his head. "Don't bother. Odds are good I won't be able to tell whether she's there to help me or kill me just from a name on a ticket."

His friend sighed. "That's true enough. This whole mission is a question mark. It might be a trap. It might not. She might have intel about The Serpent she wants to share with you, though God only knows why. Or she could be someone in your line of work, and she's coming to the island to kill you. Hell, maybe The Serpent screwed her, too, and she wants to kill him and hopes you'll team up with her."

"Only way I'll know is to go," Tony said without hesitation, because the trip became a done deal the moment The-Asst had suggested it. After all, he'd risked his life for things a lot more mundane than his own lifetime vendetta.

"Figured you'd say that. You'll need to go in as a couple. You seeing anyone these days? Anyone you'd be willing to take on a mission?"

"No on both counts," Tony admitted, ignoring the tug on his heart that came with the admission.

Noah watched him for a moment, those deep green eyes never leaving Tony's face. "It's not so bad, buddy. Honestly, it's pretty damn good."

That tug turned into a downright squeeze as he silently shrugged. He was doing just fine, at least so long as he lived in the moment. It was only hard when the dark, lonely nights came, a reminder that he couldn't ever truly get close to anyone because that would be like painting a target on their ass, then—

Fuck.

He grabbed the mug of now-cold coffee and

took a long swallow, just to camouflage his souring mood.

"I'm happy for you," he told Noah after he set the mug down with a thunk. "I really am." He smiled, the expression genuine as he remembered dinner at their house the night before. "You and Kiki are great together."

He meant it, too. Tony didn't know the whole story, but he knew that Noah had lost a wife and child, and that the tragedy had scarred him. Kiki, he knew, had helped heal those wounds.

"Yeah," Noah said, smiling so wide that Tony could see all his teeth. "We really are." He hesitated, and Tony tensed, afraid that Noah would give him the *you should settle down* speech.

Instead, Noah cleared his throat and said casually, "So who are you going to take? Or are you planning on a surreptitious arrival."

"I read a bit about the place. The only habitable area is the resort. Beyond that is a small, dense jungle. There's a road to and from the airport, but that's about it. So if I'm going to the island, I'm going to the resort."

"And you need a woman. Got one in mind?"

"I don't. Anyone I take, I put at risk." And even if that wasn't the case, he didn't have anyone in mind. While he'd picked up a few women here and there, those hadn't been the kind of encounters where he'd kept a phone number. And as for women with the kind of skill set to be a partner and not a decoration? Well, his contact list was short as he preferred working alone and had been fully solo since Deliverance disbanded.

"You need someone who can hold her own," Noah said.

"Agreed. But who?"

His friend shook his head. "No ideas. I've been riding a desk for too long now, and my contacts have dried up. I wish I could point you somewhere."

"I do, too. I need someone connected. Someone who has a large pool to—of course." He smiled. "Stark."

"Stark?" Noah repeated. "As in my boss? Damien Stark of Stark Applied Technology?"

"And the Stark Security Agency," Tony reminded him. After his daughter was kidnapped, Damien Stark founded the elite security group to go after scum like the kidnapper—and worse. The goal of the SSA, as Damien had told him, was to be a line in the sand. To fight the battles that law enforcement couldn't—or wouldn't—and to help those who might otherwise fall through the cracks.

The SSA was relatively new, but it had already earned a stellar reputation. And though Tony had declined Stark's offer to join the team, that didn't mean that he didn't respect the hell out of its mission or its operatives.

"Good idea," Noah said, nodding slowly. "You want me to give him a call and see if any of the women on the team are free for a job? Or, hell, Liam and Quincy are both with the SSA," he added, referring to two other former Deliverance members. "You could hit either of them up to approach Stark."

"No worries. I'll call him myself."

Noah's eyes widened, and Tony had to chuckle. Tony had learned that Stark was a hell of a nice guy, but there was no denying the billionaire was intimidating as hell. And Noah had no way of knowing that Tony had met Stark on multiple occasions—and that Stark had been actively recruiting him.

"He owes me a favor," Tony explained.

Noah leaned back, clearly intrigued. "That's a hell of a chip to be holding."

"Yeah, well, let's just say he thinks I'm worth it. I helped his wife out of a jam in Paris a while back."

An attacker had gone after Nikki and, thankfully, Tony had been in the right place at the right time.

"Stark said to give him a shout if I ever needed anything. Guess I'll call in the favor and tell him I need a woman."

CHAPTER TWO

I'm hanging upside down outside the window of one of Burbank's hotels, and I can't help but think that the world looks pretty much the same from twenty-four floors above the ground as it does right-side up at sea level.

But then, I'm not a sunshine and roses kind of girl. On the contrary, I've always thought that the world was a fucked up place, as often upside-down and backwards as it is safe and navigable. No, that's not true. It's more often fucked up. The warm and cozy world that you see on television commercials? That everyone's grandmother claims to remember? It doesn't really exist. I don't think it ever really did.

Harsh, maybe. But the truth usually is.

I first learned about harsh realities when I

was still in diapers. I didn't have a stellar child-hood, that's for sure, but my perspective on the world gave me an edge. And my interesting string of jobs over the years has given me some very unique skill sets. The kind of expertise a woman needs if she plans on gathering a shit-ton of compromising intel from a money laun-dering asshole who, once upon a time, also brokered the sale of little girls on the black market.

Unfortunately for me, Billy Cane isn't an easy guy to get close to. Which explains why I'm hanging upside down in front of his hotel window, a cable and a reinforced harness keeping me in place, as I try to hold my camera steady while I zoom in on his computer where he's doing some very naughty things.

Not sexual things, though.

There are no scantily clad prostitutes in my view. No revelations into Mr. Billy Cane's personal predilections. I'm not trying to catch him in that kind of compromising position. I'm trying to catch him moving money. Lots of money for lots of underworld clients.

I want to capture the keystrokes. I want shiny footage of the account numbers. I want all the juicy details. Because the more info I have to bargain with, the less likely anyone is going to care that I popped the guy.

Because that, of course, is the real reason I'm here.

A crackle of static in my earpiece catches my attention, then Quincy's smooth British vowels fill my head. "Status, Auntie?" It's a silly call sign, but protocol requires no names over the radio. The code name comes from Auntie Em of the *Wizard of Oz*, one of my favorite movies. And since I'm Emma, it's a name I choose often for missions.

"Five-by-five. Just enjoying the view."

"As much fun as waiting to reel you in might be, this mission is a bit below my pay grade."

Quincy Radcliffe is not only one of the Stark Security Agency's first recruits, he's also a former Deliverance operative and a former MI6 agent. Which means he's absolutely right. "Feeling extraneous?"

"You said you needed me specifically," he reminds me. "And you asked me to bring company equipment even though you're not with us."

"I practically am." The company is the Stark Security Agency, Quincy's current employer.

"Are you, now? Do go on. When you asked

me, I had the impression you'd be signing on the dotted line any day now. And yet I don't believe you've signed a bloody thing."

I almost smile. "You sounded seriously fucking British right then."

"I am seriously fucking British. I'm also the man who is going to decide when and if I'm going to reel you up again. I want a straight bloody answer. Did you sign on to the company?"

If I weren't hanging upside down, I'd shrug. "Technically, no."

Damien Stark's been asking me to come on board as an operative with the elite security agency ever since I rescued a kidnapped princess and Quince helped take down the fuckwad who was after her.

I admire the heck out of the SSA, but I also like my freedom. Working on my own terms. I spent too many years as a covert op for a deep-cover government intelligence organization. Under the circumstances, that was a kickass deal for me. A hell of a lot better than death row, that's for damn sure.

Now that I'm no longer yoked to the government, my freedom is important to me. Quince knows it. My sister knows it. I know it.

I'm still trying to figure out if Stark Security knows it.

"Explain *not exactly*," he demands.

"Well, you're here, and you're part of the company, and you're my sister's boyfriend. That's way less than six degrees of separation. You do the math."

His beleaguered sigh fills my ear, and I have to smile. Right now—upside down and all—I'm having one hell of a good time.

"Which begs the question of why I agreed to your absurd request in the first place."

Through the crack in the hotel room's curtain, I see Cane shift in his chair, revealing even more of the computer screen. I grin, then zoom in for a much better image of the spreadsheet he's editing, chockfull of names and account numbers. "That's it, you fucker. And thank you for being so anally organized."

"Auntie..."

"Fine, fine. I'm assuming you agreed because you're screwing my sister. God knows that was a big part of why I asked you."

"Trust me. As much as I adore that particular activity, it wouldn't be enough."

"Then it must be because you love my sister."

"Ah, yes. That's why."

"She's lucky to have you," I tell him. "And I'm not just saying that because you could push a lever and drop me on my head."

"I'm lucky to have her."

"Damn right, you are."

"And right now, you're lucky to have me."

I laugh softly. "Can't argue with that one either."

"Care to give me a bit more information about what exactly you're doing? Nature of the intel? Your mission objective?"

"Nope."

"Because I might tell your sister?"

"Yup."

"You know she'd—"

"*Hang on.*"

The bastard is pushing back from the desk, and it's clear why—my own reflection right there on his goddamn computer screen. *Dammit, dammit, dammit.*

I wanted more footage. Lots more.

But I'll have to make do with what I have, because it's now or never time. And I'm not willing to stop now.

I do a quick flip in the harness, shifting my position to right-side up, then use the clip at the top of the harness to hook me into this position.

These aren't ideal conditions, but when are they ever?

I grab the Smith & Wesson .45 that's holstered to my hip, say a prayer that the wind doesn't shift, and quickly take aim. I've done this before, albeit not while suspended, but I'd always been assigned a partner on those missions. One of us to shoot out the glass, the other to almost simultaneously shoot the target, thus eliminating the need to account for the deflection of the kill shot when it penetrates the pane.

But I don't have a partner beside me, and I don't have time for hefty calculations. And while I'll aim for a kill shot the first time, most likely I'll have to take the second shot on its heels. If it works, great. If not, I damn sure hope Quince can haul my ass to the roof before Cane takes a shot at me.

Time seems to drag on dangerously slow, but that's an illusion. The world is moving in slo-mo now. My thoughts coming at such a fast clip that he's not even fully steady on his feet yet. But I've got the weapon ready, and the moment he's upright and facing me, I fire. The glass shatters, and he's close enough to get sprayed by the shards.

Flying glass can be deadly, but I'm not

willing to take a chance, and the glass is still flying when I take aim, pull the trigger again, and send the bullet zinging through the newly formed hole in the window. And right into that son-of-a-bitch's head.

I rattle off an ironic curse. Ironic because though I'd been aiming for his chest, I nailed the more difficult shot. Even so, I hate it when subpar conditions fuck with my aim.

I draw a breath, calm myself, and tell Quince to pull me the hell back up.

Immediately, I start to move up, and at a pretty fast clip. But that's also when I realize that he hasn't said a word. Yeah. He's pissed.

"Listen, Bond," I say, using this call sign. Because, hey, he's British. "This was—"

"*Bloody hell*," Quince growls. At first I think he's even more pissed than I anticipated, but a split second later, I start to free fall and realize he's dealing with an equipment fuck-up.

The clip holding me upright isn't designed to withstand intense pressure, and when I jerk a few feet above Cane's room, I also spin forward, the air coming out of my lungs with a *whoosh*. Suddenly I'm upside down again, staring through the glass into Cane's room.

He's still there, still dead, and still alone.

There are no sirens. No sign that anyone at three in the morning noticed the shower of glass that rained down on the parking lot below. And no indication that hotel security is racing to his room.

I do have a problem, though. Because when I flipped, the camera shifted. Now it's hanging from my arm, tethered only by the strap I'm wearing across my body.

Considering I'm currently upside down, this isn't the most secure of positions. "What the hell are you doing up there?" I demand.

"Got a jam in the recoil system. Give me a —*there.*"

His final word is unnecessary, because I can hardly miss the fact that I'm now zooming upward, the crank's motor having obviously re-engaged.

The camera starts to fall, but it can't go far because the strap is around my body.

Except that it's not. I realize too late that the metal clip that attaches the strap to one side of the camera has come loose—and now the weight of the camera is pulling the damn thing free faster than I can scramble for it.

"Goddammit," I snarl as my fingers brush the end of the strap, but I can't get a grip. And I watch, helpless, as the camera tumbles through the night to smash unseen on the dark parking lot below.

There's a chance—a slim one—that the SD card survived. But I'm not holding my breath. Instead, I growl into the mic. "Tell me the wifi was working. Tell me you got the image transfer."

"No glitches," Quince assures me. "I'll confirm the images were transferred once you're up here. Can you see where it landed?"

"More or less. We'll retrieve it when we exit the scene." A moment later, my feet have reached the barrier that marks the edge of the roof. I pike up and re-orient myself with my head up, as if I'm some sort of trapeze artist.

I grab hold of the ledge around the roof and pull myself up and over in time to see him standing beside the now-locked crank, his attention on the tablet in front of him.

"Got them. Let's go."

To his credit, he says nothing else as we pack the equipment in seconds, then use the utility elevator to get to the basement. We exit through a service entrance, both keeping our heads down and shielded by black, generic baseball caps.

Only after we've retrieved the broken camera, confirmed the images transferred safe and sound to the remote tablet, and are miles away in the plain, black Toyota—without license plates—does Quincy turn to me and say, "What the bloody hell is going on?"

He's driving, and he pulls into a deserted bank parking lot. I don't even grimace. It's not like I wasn't expecting this.

"It's personal," I tell him. "And sanctioned. Don't worry. There won't be blowback."

"Sanctioned," he repeats. "But not by my company." He kills the engine and looks at me, his expression as hard as glass. He glances to the backseat where our gear, including one of Stark Security's tablets, are safe and sound in a go-bag. "I'm assuming the photos are important and you weren't just practicing your artistic composition skills before taking out the guy."

I cock my head, not even bothering to answer.

"So here's what happens. Tell me what this is all about, and I'll get the images for you. Keep me in the dark, and you'll have to steal the bloody tablet and hack the passcode. And no offense, but I don't think you're that good with tech. I'm not sure anyone is. The SSA has serious security. You might find someone to eventually hack it, but I wouldn't want to take those odds."

"Quince." Over the years, I've cultivated a firm and intimidating voice. Unfortunately, my sister's boyfriend isn't the type to be intimidated.

"No." His voice is harsh. No nonsense. This is the man who withstood torture. The man who saved my sister. And the man who now protects her, just like I once did.

I feel my resolve shift.

"This isn't an SSA mission," he continues. "And despite suggesting as much when you asked me to come with you, you aren't actually on the cusp of joining the SSA, are you?"

I say nothing.

"Fine. Tell me what the fuck's going on, or this whole exercise was for nothing."

"Eliza said you were a principled hard-ass."

"She knows me well. Talk."

"It's personal. Me and Eliza."

"That makes it personal to me, too."

"Oh? Have you proposed?"

His mouth twitches and even in the dim ambient light I can actually see the hint of color rising up his neck.

"Oh my God. You *did* propose. I can't believe she didn't tell me."

"Not yet. But soon. I have the ring in my pocket."

"Your pocket," I repeat. "Here? Now?"

He lifts a shoulder. "Until it's on her finger, I'm not letting it out of my sight. And even then, I'm not letting it get too far away."

I feel my heart melt a little, which is not a common feeling for me. Yes, I've been known to tear up during the occasional sappy film when my sister forces me to watch them, but on the whole, relationships and the mess that goes with them really aren't my thing.

Sure, I've had a few friends with benefits over the years, but that's sex and laughs and a good time. Nothing serious. Because what's the point? I've got Eliza. I've got my circle. And that's plenty. The world's a harsh enough place as it is, and the more you get close, the more you get vulnerable.

Still, I'm happy for Eliza. She's practically floated through life ever since she and Quince got together again after a particularly bad parting many years ago.

He's since redeemed himself a hundred-fold. And since he had a significant hand in saving my life and the princess, I have to admit I'm predisposed to liking the guy again.

Most important, I know he loves her.

"The mission," he presses.

I hesitate, then nod. He came tonight to help me, no questions asked. And, yes, I might have suggested that Stark was okay with it, but I know damn well he didn't believe it. Not when the briefing consisted of the two of us discussing mission specs in my Jeep outside a Taco Bell.

And, yeah, I sort of forgot to mention the part about my plan to kill Cane.

Bottom line, he deserves to know. And I should probably get used to the fact that Quincy Radcliffe is family, too.

Family. What a weird fucking word. When I was little, I thought it meant blood and birth and genealogical shit. DNA and genes.

But that's bullshit. Blood isn't family. Not the kind of family that counts.

"Our father was planning to sell us," I tell him, surprised that the furious noise in my head translated to a whisper in the dark.

I see the pain cross his face, but there's no surprise. I already know that Eliza has told him our story. And while she never knew that particular vile plan of daddy dearest, I guess it's not a shock when you know about the rest of the evil that clung to that man.

"I never told Eliza, but I'll understand if you tell her now. I know you two don't like having secrets, and I probably should have told her long ago."

He shakes his head. "She didn't need to know, and you were doing what you've done your whole life. Taking care of her." He reaches out and casually brushes my hand. "It doesn't change a thing, but I want you to know it matters to me."

I nod, then realize I'm looking down because there are tears in my eyes, which makes no sense whatsoever. Or maybe it does. Because he loves who I love, and that's a good thing.

"So Cane was the buyer?"

I shake my head. "No, that was someone else. An entitled prick with fingers in industries both legitimate and not. But he's dead."

"And Cane was the next best thing."

I nod. "He brokered the deal. He brokered a lot of deals. Still does."

He nods slowly. "You should have told me before."

"Would you have come with me?"

"Of course."

I shrug. "Then what's the difference?"

He rubs his temples. "Emma..." He trails off, then rubs his temples again. "Of course I would have helped. You know what I've done. Who I've worked for."

I nod. He was with MI6 and with Deliverance, a vigilante group that was formed to take out men just like Cane and rescue kidnapping victims.

"You don't have to always work alone," he says.

"I don't. There's Lorenzo. There've been others." When I worked as a PI, I partnered with an ex-cop. Lorenzo had helped get me and Eliza off the streets. But the truth is, even when we worked together on cases, we had our own separate threads to follow. Most of the time, like Quince said, I work alone. I like it that way.

"You know this could get messy. I would have helped. But you should have kept me in the loop. When cops get involved ... if this somehow comes back to us..."

"It won't."

His brow furrows.

"The site will be clean by morning. And if the body's discovered before then, it'll be covered up. There won't be blowback."

He's silent for a moment. He knows who I used to work for, the kind of connections I have. "You wanted to take out Cane. And the government wanted to know who he was laundering money for."

"You're a smart guy, Mr. Bond."

He waits for me to say more, but I stay silent. He knows the score. I think he even understands what drives me.

I didn't change the past by killing Cane, but I think I did get justice. At least a little.

Eliza deserves that. And so, I think, do I.

CHAPTER THREE

I sit on the edge of the infinity pool, looking out over the hills of Malibu and the Pacific Ocean beyond. This isn't my first time in Damien Stark's backyard, but I never get tired of this view.

Why would I? It's everything I didn't have as a kid. I'd grown up in a shithole of a house, nothing like this. I'd shared a windowless basement room with my little sister, courtesy of our prick of a father. A man we'd escaped when I was fifteen and Eliza was eight. A man who didn't care about pretty views or his children or anything other than himself, his pervy urges, and the cheap whiskey he guzzled by the gallon.

Bastard.

Abusive, rank, lowlife, dead bastard.

I've done a lot of things in my life. Some pretty damn dicey. But they all led to this. To a life that's clean and, for the most part, safe. For myself, sure, but mostly for Eliza.

I glance around out of habit to find her. Even though she's grown, and even though we're often physically apart, I can't seem to stop looking out for her. I see her with Quince, her gleaming mahogany hair falling around her shoulders and the hem of a sundress fluttering in the wind around her knees.

At her side, Quince is decked out in a faded blue tee and threadbare jeans. He looks nothing like the black clad partner who saved my ass from dropping twenty-four floors to the concrete two nights ago. And not just his clothes. No, on our mission he'd been all business. Now, he looks like a man in love.

And despite all my years of being the most important person in Eliza's life, I'm not only okay with that, I'm genuinely happy for her.

For me, too, actually. Eliza and I never had a family. Hell, we never had close friends. There's Lorenzo, the partner in the private investigation firm I own. Or, rather, *owned*. Past tense now that I've sold him my interest. But that's about it.

Now Eliza has Quince and all of the folks

at Stark Security and all of the folks in their circle. And now I get the benefit of the overflow, too.

Which is why I'm here at a party celebrating Dallas and Jane Sykes and their new baby. A couple I don't really know, though I've read enough about them online and in the papers over the years. Hard to avoid news about a playboy heir who ends up marrying his sister.

"Hey."

I jump at the sound of the voice behind me, then silently curse. Not because I don't want to talk to Cass, but because I'd been so damn relaxed that I'd let down my guard. And I *never* let down my guard.

So that's my first lesson—be a team player, sure. But don't stop checking my six.

I paste on a smile, then turn around to face my ex. Or sort of ex. The truth is, there'd never been anything more between us than a good time. Cass had been coming off of a bad breakup. And as for me...?

Well, I am who I am. I like Cass. I like sex. As far as I'd been concerned there wasn't much more to be said.

"I wasn't expecting to see you here," Cass says, stealing my line. Although honestly, I should have expected that Cass would be here in billionaire Damien Stark's backyard.

For one thing, his sister-in-law Sylvia is Cassidy Cunningham's best friend. And since this isn't a work party, it makes sense that Sylvia's here—with Cass in tow. Even if the party were an official work function for Stark Security, Cass might come as a guest. She and Denny had become good friends in the years that Denny's husband, Mason, had been gone. Denny's one of the first agents recruited for Stark Security, and damn good, too. She's also got a baby bump, and I wonder how the SSA will get along without her when she takes her leave.

A shudder runs through me as I think about all she endured. I have no desire to settle down, but that doesn't mean I can't empathize with the nightmare of having her husband go missing. And then came the cherry on that horrible sundae when he returned with absolutely no idea who she was.

The whole thing was horrifying. And maybe even one more reason not to get too attached to people. I've spent my life worrying about Eliza. And I'm honestly not sure there's room in my heart for more potential fear and pain.

And love?

The little voice comes out of nowhere and I push it down. I've somehow developed a sappy side ever since Eliza and Quince got back together, and sappy isn't a good look for me. Not at all.

"Earth to Emma."

I shake my head as if clearing cobwebs. "Sorry. Honestly, I didn't expect to see you here, either. I hope it's not awkward."

Cass dismisses my words with a wave, then slips off her sandals and sits on the edge of the pool, her feet dangling in the water, too. She looks amazing, as always. Her hair is platinum blonde today, and she wears no jewelry other than a small nose ring. Her top is sleeveless, so I can still see most of the exotic bird tattooed on her shoulder, its vibrant tail feathers cascading down her arm. "Nah, I'm good," she says. "Still friends, right?"

I meet her eyes. "Always."

"I get why you bolted. I just wish we could have talked about it."

I let a shoulder rise and fall. "It was three months ago. Water under the bridge." No way am I going to talk about my feelings. And definitely not about how Cass had messed up a perfectly good friends-with-benefits thing by suggesting we get serious. I probably should have expected it. Cass is the type who wants a steady partner. I'm not.

Cass sighs.

"What?"

"Nothing. I just hope that someday you find someone you can really talk to. Someone other than Eliza, I mean."

I keep my mouth shut. I know she means well, but so what if I don't want to get all deep and open and share my shit? That isn't who I am. It isn't who I want to be. And if I ever do need to vent, I really do have Eliza, who loves me and will always be there for me. And why can't that be enough?

"Right," Cass says, standing as my silence lingers. "You should start doing girls' night at your house again. Even if you don't invite me."

"Stopping had nothing to do with you." I used to host weekly girls' nights for the women who now surround Eliza by virtue of moving permanently to LA to be with Quincy. I'd put on my perky hostess personality and try to be bubbly. Over the years, I've developed a lot of different personalities. And it's best to keep them all in practice. After all, who knows when I'll have to become someone else for a job. Or to hide.

"Truly," I add, since Cass's expression is dubious. "I've been doing an out of town job for most of the last three months." The job had been for myself—gathering the intel on what Cane was up to so that I could go to my old boss and propose the hit. In exchange for covering for me, the SOC would get the intel I gathered about Cane's clients. "Since Eliza's picked up the slack, I didn't think to start having them at my house again."

"Fair enough," Cass says. "I just wanted to make sure we were good."

"We are. Totally."

Cass frowns and I almost sigh. Surely we're not going to have to go another round of touchy-feely talk. But then she says, "Check that out."

I realize the frown is meant for something behind me, and I turn, then draw in a sharp breath when I see him.

Not that I know him, the guy with the dark hair, haunted eyes, and just enough beard stubble to give him a cavalier edge. I don't know why, but something about him seriously pushes my buttons. "Nice," I say. "Who is he?" He's talking with Damien, so I assume he must be a party guest.

"His name's Antonio Santos."

"You know him?"

Cass shakes her head. "I was nearby when he came in. The guard working the garden entrance asked for his name and ID before calling Damien."

"Interesting," I say, and Cass laughs.

"What's funny?"

A grin tugs at her mouth. "I'm just relieved. We really must be out of the weirdness and back in the friend zone if you're going gaga over some guy while you're standing right next to me."

"Not gaga. Just admiring the view."

"Not bad, but I'm not interested," Cass says. "He's not my type. Note the pronoun."

I purposefully let my gaze roam over the specimen. "Personally, I'm all about equal opportunity"

Cass rolls her eyes. "Come on. If we go get a drink we'll walk right past him. You can do that sexy thing with your eyes. Maybe he'll bite. I'm sure Damien won't mind if you try to pick up one of his guests."

"I don't do a thing with my eyes."

"Yeah. You do. Come on."

I consider arguing about the eye thing, but don't. As for the walk, I'm totally down for that. And not because I want to make eyes at the guy. I'm simply glad I don't have to walk on eggshells around Cass.

Unfortunately, we've only gone a few feet when Damien and Antonio Santos turn and walk down one of the long paths that meanders through the property. I stand still for a moment, realizing with annoyance that I'm more disappointed than I should be.

"So we'll get a drink anyway?" Cass asks.

"Sounds good to me." Right now, I could use one.

We're almost to the bar when Quince joins us. He stands beside me, but he talks to Cass. "Can I borrow her?"

I look at Cass, who shrugs. "Okay," I tell Quince, then look at Cass. "I'll catch up with you later?"

"Sure. I'll be around here somewhere."

Once she wanders off, I tilt my head and wait for what I know Quince is going to say.

"You joined Stark Security, despite suggesting to me two days ago on a certain rooftop that you had absolutely no interest in joining the team. For that matter, considering the mission, I would have been justified in thinking you were going back to the SOC."

"Disappointed?"

He actually glowers. "As a matter of fact, I'm thrilled. You're a hell of an asset, and you've made your sister very happy. But I'm a bit cheesed off you kept me in the dark."

I consider giving him a brush-off answer, but decide on the truth. He deserves it. "You were a test case."

He says nothing, but it's clear from his expression that he expects me to continue.

"I like my freedom, okay? But I also admire talent and loyalty. And a bit of the rebel and rule-breaker mixed in doesn't turn me off, okay? And Stark's offer really was generous, and it's a great team, so—"

"So basically, you took the SSA for a test drive through me."

"Pretty much," I admit.

He considers that. "Well, then I have to thank you."

My brow furrows. "Why?"

"Because I can imagine how excited Eliza will be when she hears that I played such a huge part in gaining your agreement. I intend to take advantage of that."

There's a devilish twinkle in his gray eyes, and I put my hands over my ears. "I don't even want to know about your raunchy plans with my sister."

"Raunchy?" Eliza's amused voice comes from behind, and I turn to see her grinning. Not at me, but at Quince. "Care to elaborate?"

"Don't you dare," I say, fighting a laugh as Quince lifts a hand as if he's about to count off five wildly sexual things he has planned for my little sister.

We all grin, and Eliza slides into his arms and tilts her head up for a quick kiss. Once again, I feel that unexpected tightening in my chest. I tell myself it's just melancholy. Like the way a mom feels when her daughter gets married and the girl is no longer hers alone.

"I can't believe you didn't tell me about joining the SSA," Eliza says, after she breaks the kiss with a sigh.

"A girl's gotta have some secrets."

"And now I have to take her to see Damien," Quince says. "Grab me a drink and I'll meet you back here?"

"You got it." She flashes an impish grin at me. "Already in trouble with the boss?"

"Go," I say. "Pest."

She laughs, then skips away, her fingers brushing Quincy's until they're far enough apart that contact is impossible.

"You two are good together."

"That we are. Come on."

I follow, basking in the love I hear for my sister. Though I tried hard to make it okay, there's no escaping the reality of our shitty childhood. Eliza deserves to be happy, and I'm glad they found each other.

I mentally shake my head, clearing the emotional baggage. Right now, I either need to be joining in the fete for the Sykes' new baby or wondering about why Stark wants to see me. I focus on the latter. "I talked to Damien and Ryan earlier when I accepted the job. What's up now?" While Damien Stark founded Stark Security, Ryan Hunter runs it.

"Haven't a clue. He just asked if I'd track you down. This is me, following orders. Not a rebellious bone in my body."

"Funny man," I say, following him toward the house with a rising feeling of dread. The only reason for Stark to want to see me is to give me an assignment—in which case he'd most likely wait until Monday—or because he's found out about my Thursday night excursion with Quince. And since Quince and I will be heading into the Starks' Malibu mansion together, I'm guessing we're in for a dressing down.

And by *we*, I mean me.

As it turns out, we don't go inside. Instead, we veer around the incredible home on a path that leads to the professional quality tennis court. Not that I'm an expert on courts, but since Damien used to play professionally, I figure it's a reasonable guess. He's sitting at a small table just inside the fenced area, and Antonio Santos is right beside him, his stubbled chin resting on a fist as he studies me.

I shift my weight from foot to foot. I'm not usually self-conscious, but something about the way he's examining me has me resisting the urge to stand up taller. Instead, I make sure my posture is casual as I regard him with equal intensity.

He doesn't flinch. Not even when Damien has to repeat himself to catch Antonio's attention. Only then does he glance away before nodding in response to whatever Damien said.

Then he's back to focusing on me as Damien heads in my direction, crossing the court until he's standing right in front of us.

Damien looks between Quince and me, and

I'm certain he's going to dress us down about the operation at the hotel. But all Damien says is, "Thanks for showing Emma to the court. I can take it from here."

From the surprise I see flicker over Quince's face, I can tell he expected at least a slap on the wrist. But he gives me a *you're on* look, waves at Antonio who's still at the table, then walks off, prompting me to realize I'd missed an opportunity. Apparently Quincy knows the guy. And I would very much have liked at least a clue as to who Santos is.

"I spoke with Anderson," Damien says, and it takes me a minute to interpret that sentence.

"Colonel Seagrave." The name falls unnecessarily from my lips. Of course, that's who Damien's talking about. My former boss and mentor at the Sensitive Operations Command where I'd worked as an agent—really, a ghost—for a good part of my life. The man to whom I'd promised Cane's list in exchange for a James Bond style license to kill the little son of a bitch.

"I told him you'd signed on with us."

I feel the tension leave my body. I'd been expecting a sharp lecture about utilizing SSA resources without SSA authorization. "I was going to let him know today. He knows I've been considering it for a while."

"He was pleased. But I got the impression from our conversation that you worked solo for the SOC."

"Does that come as a surprise?"

"No. But I do want to reiterate that our policy at the SSA is for agents to work primarily in teams. There are exceptions, but I'm not interested in building an organization full of loners. The work the SSA does is serious and sensitive. Everyone on staff needs to know and trust each other—agents, tech, clerical, all the way down to housekeeping. There's no room for a lone wolf in my shop."

"I thought it was Ryan's shop."

I'm right, and I know it. Damien Stark runs a multinational, multibillion-dollar empire, and from what I've read, he's pretty hands-on about all his enterprises. But he isn't an agent and has no background in law enforcement. He's not someone who checks in day to day at the SSA. And that, in fact, is why he put Ryan Hunter in charge, a man with a long list of law enforcement and intelligence credentials.

So, yeah. My statement was right. Even so, I

cringe when Damien says, "My name is on the door, Emma. It's my shop."

"Of course," I say, then add, "Sir."

His shoulders relax and he drags his fingers through his hair. "That's not necessary either. All I want to do is make a point about team work and communication." He looks hard at me, and I look right back at him, not blinking.

The truth is, he's right and I know it. But I spent too many years doing exactly what the government big shots said without question or objection because they held my life—and, by extension, Eliza's life—in their hands. Years of following orders. Of doing what I was told and only what I was told.

Eventually I got some leeway, sure. With my skillset, they allowed me that. And maybe there was a bit of trust there, too, at the end. I don't know. All I know is that I was nothing but a toy for my father and then a puppet for the government. When I finally got clear and opened my own shop and started calling my own shots, the freedom was heady.

And deep down, I'm really not sure that agreeing to join Stark Security was the best plan.

Correction—that's not a deep down fear. That's a right under the surface fear. I've almost pulled the plug so many times, and yet something keeps pulling me toward this group. Something more than Eliza's connection. Just because her man is an agent doesn't mean I need to be one, too.

No, the truth is, I've seen how competent they are, not to mention how many resources are at the agents' disposal. And there is a lot of appeal to being part of a group that does good work. I've been telling myself that for months. I think I even finally believe it. Hell, I accepted the job. God knows the pay took some of the sting out of the decision.

But still, I've had these niggling doubts. And now they've become a little more than niggling since I'm already getting this subtle dressing down for my first mission. Which, of course, wasn't really a mission. And which, of course, broke all of the SSA's rules.

"You get what I'm saying, right?" Stark continues. "No secret missions. No hidden vendettas. We expect it. *I* expect it."

I nod, but I already know I'll break those rules if I have to. If it's something personal—like to protect Eliza or myself from a ghost from our past—I'm not pulling the SSA into my shit. Fortunately, now that Cane's dead, the last ties to the nightmare of our childhood have been severed. Now, I'm all about the job someone pays me for. And if the Stark Security Agency is footing the bill, then I'm an open book.

"I get it," I say.

"Good. Other than that, we have only one firm policy."

"And that is?"

"Do a damn good job."

"I always do."

He smiles, and I see the man who has so often charmed the world. "That's why we hired you."

"Is this about my first official SSA job? Are you partnering me with Santos?"

He glances over my shoulder at the man. "No. And yes."

I say nothing, just wait for him to explain.

"He's not with the SSA. But I do owe him a favor. He has a meeting scheduled with an informant on the Debauchery Resort. But he can't get in—"

"—without a woman." I nod, trying to mask my annoyance—not to mention the fears that I jumped too quickly to join this team. I thought they wanted me for my skills. Instead, I'm accompanying someone who isn't even with the SSA on a trip so that I can be arm candy?

"Is that a problem?"

"Actually, it is." I cross my arms and shift my stance. "I thought you hired me because I'm all kinds of good at my job. But instead you're pawning me off on some civilian who needs an escort?"

"First of all, I'm not pawning you off. And second, I'm very aware of your skill set. You demonstrated some of those skills last night, very skillfully utilizing a litany of equipment you had Quince pull from SSA inventory."

"So this is a hand slap. You're upset I didn't get permission and so now I'm being punished and shoved into a bikini? Come on, Stark I got enough of that kind of petty game-playing working for the government."

"Emma, that's not what this is."

"I know exactly what this is." Who am I fooling thinking I can join this big family that Stark's spouting off about? I can't. I know it. And I should have known better than to even try.

"This is a mistake," I continue. "And you know what, Stark? If you owe him the favor, then you put on the fucking bikini. I'm out."

The words are out before I can call them back, but maybe it's for the best. And so with that total career bomb still echoing across the court, I turn on my heel, shoot Antonio Santos a half-angry, half-apologetic look, and march straight off the tennis court toward my car.

CHAPTER FOUR

Tony tried to keep a straight face as he crossed the court toward Stark, but it wasn't easy. He wasn't sure if he was amused, turned on, or just impressed as hell. But he knew one thing for certain—Emma Tucker had some serious *cojones*.

"I'll talk to Ryan about recalling Leah. She doesn't have as much field work under her belt, but she's smart and trained and—"

Tony held up a hand. "I want Emma."

Damien raised a brow, and Tony looked into those oddly hypnotic dual-colored eyes. "As you just saw, I can hardly force her. For that matter, I'm not certain I still employ her."

"She's ballsy. She can hold her own. And I

don't have a clue what I'm really walking into. Could be an easy meet and an exchange of info. Or I might end up with a gun aimed at my head." He crossed his arms as he shifted his weight from one foot to the other.

Damien nodded, his expression thoughtful. "I told you in Paris that I owe you one, and I meant it. But I can't compel her. And I won't try. That's not the way I work."

"I get it. I wouldn't want you to. As far as I'm concerned, you've satisfied the obligation."

"I'm not sure—"

"I am," Tony said. "I walked into this party and told you I needed a woman. You found me the perfect partner for this job in under an hour. You did your part," he added with a shrug.

"I'm happy to find you another partner for the job," Stark said. "Where you're concerned, I'm inclined to go over and above. I want you on the team."

"Then you know how I feel about Emma. I want her, Stark. And I'm going to get her."

———

Tony pulled his hybrid Land Rover into the

narrow driveway of Emma's Venice Beach house, thankful that Quince had vouched for him with her sister.

"You're not going to get anywhere with her," Eliza had told him. "Emma's stubborn, and she makes her own rules. She always has. And it sounds like she's made up her mind." Her mouth twitched. "Once she's dug in, there's no digging her out. But if you want to waste your time, be my guest," she'd added, then rattled off the address.

Now Tony was here, and he sat for a moment with the SUV in park, mournful blues filling the car from the ridiculously awesome sound system he'd installed a month after he bought the thing. He intended to take a moment to hone his plan to convince her.

He never got the chance. His thoughts were interrupted by a sharp rapping at his window, and there she stood. The plain silver band she wore on her right hand clacked against the glass, and he looked into her stern expression, her hazel eyes dull and expressionless.

Stark had told him she was a pro, and one look at her face proved it.

He hadn't yet killed the engine, so he hit the button to roll down the window. "Problem?"

"What the hell are you doing in my driveway? Did Stark actually give you my address?"

"I asked, but he refused. I got it from Eliza," he added, since that was a nice, subtle way to suggest that her sister was on his side.

"Oh, for fuck's sake."

He expected her to say more. To tell him to get off the property. Or that he should explain why he was there. Something.

But all she did was turn around and walk back into the house.

For a moment he simply sat there, looking at the spot where she'd been. Then he realized that he was smiling. This woman was turning out to be a hell of a lot of trouble. But he also had a feeling that she was worth it.

He killed the engine, got out of the vehicle, and followed the path to the blue door of her charming little bungalow.

She opened it before he reached the patio. "You don't give up easily, do you?"

"You wouldn't want to work with me if I did."

Her voice held no irony as she said, "I don't want to work with you now."

"Yeah," he said. "You do."

He waited for her to slam the door in his face.

Instead, she opened it wider. "Convince me," she said, and invited him in.

He stepped into the tiled entry hall, then followed her into the spacious living room filled with both light and comfortable-looking furniture. The walls were wood and stone, and were covered in colorful paintings and framed photographs. A bookcase took up one wall, and he stifled the urge to study the spines, just to see what Emma Tucker read. He didn't, but only because she was already in the next room, and he hurried to catch up to her in the kitchen.

"Great house. You own or rent?"

"I bought it years ago," she said. "It was a dump. I made improvements."

That was obvious in the kitchen, which had very clearly been expanded. He guessed that she'd sacrificed what was probably a bedroom to make room for a huge granite island, a roomy prep area, and a dining section well-lit from the late afternoon sun that streamed in through huge windows, beyond which he could see a tiny, flower-filled yard.

He took it all in, trying to reconcile the neat-but-lived-in kitchen, the flowers, and the streaming sunshine with the personality he'd built out in his head. It didn't quite compute.

"You look befuddled," she said, nodding for him to take a seat at one of the stools by the island. "Coffee? Wine? Whiskey? Something else entirely?"

"Whatever you're having. And I'm not befuddled. I'm just reprocessing."

She reached into a cabinet and pulled out a bottle of Charbay Release III, and though he tried not to react, he was certain his eyes widened. He happened to know that particular bottle cost upwards of four-hundred dollars.

The corner of her mouth twitched as she lifted a shoulder then poured him a shot, neat. She slid it toward him. "I figure you deserve the good stuff. You came all this way for nothing, after all."

"Not for nothing," he countered, then nodded at the glass. "I got the good stuff, didn't I?"

As he'd hoped, she laughed. He was starting to figure out Emma Tucker, he thought. Take it slow. Take it honest. If he couldn't be real, don't be anything at all.

At least, that was his plan for the moment. He had the sneaking suspicion that she'd continue to surprise him. And damned if he didn't like that about the woman.

Across the island from him, she hopped up on the counter by the sink, her legs dangling. He hadn't been that far behind her coming here, but she'd already changed clothes. Now she wore leggings and a form fitting tank top. And, yeah, he'd noticed the curves as he'd followed her through the house. He had eyes, after all.

But he'd also noticed her strength. The subtle tightening of muscles as she pulled herself up. There was a toughness about her. Some of it visible in her physique and the fact that she was obviously in shape. But mostly it was in the way she held herself. As if she could take down a man with a harsh look—and if that didn't work, she'd land a solid kick to his head and lay him out for good.

Strength and power. That was the Emma Tucker he saw in this kitchen with flowers beyond the windows, herbs growing in pots on the sill above the sink, and kitchen towels decorated with cartoon-style cupcakes.

To completely round out the contradiction, the toes of her bare feet were painted pink. And her practical ponytail was softened by the wisps of red hair that framed her lovely face.

"Like what you see?"

There was a challenge in her voice, but he didn't try to dodge. Instead, he simply said, "What's not to like?"

She burst out laughing. Score one for the home team.

"I'm not going with you to some island to make goo-goo eyes at you while my tits are falling out of a bikini."

"Not a problem. We'll make sure the bikini fits properly. And goo-goo eyes aren't necessary. Just a few adoring glances should do the trick nicely."

She almost laughed again. He could tell by the way she held her mouth firmly closed, keeping it back. Too bad. She had a hell of a nice laugh.

"You surprise me," she said.

"Then we're even. You surprise me, too."

"Do I? How?" She leaned forward, the position revealing an enticing bit of cleavage, and his body responded in a way that made him remember that he'd been celibate for going on four months now.

"Yo. Antonio. Up here."

He looked up, ignoring the embarrassment of getting caught and going instead for brutal honesty when he said, "Just one more reason to convince you to come with me. It would suck if I had to escort a woman who did nothing for me."

"Nice save. Now tell me how I surprise you. Other than my cleavage, that is."

"Your house. I mean, your hand towels not only have cupcakes on them, they match the oven mitts."

"Sweet of you to notice."

"And for someone with your reputation and history, I'm surprised how accessible this place is. The front door is solid, but it's just wood, and there's a vertical window beside it, albeit shuttered. You have a back door off the living room and off the kitchen. And that wall of windows? Anyone wants in here, you're not keeping them out."

"Aren't I?"

He glanced around more, looking for hidden security cameras. He didn't see any, but he was certain they were there. "You can't monitor the place twenty-four/seven. To be honest, I expected a fortress."

"Like Stark's place? I don't have the luxury of buying acres and acres. Especially considering I like living here. I've been in Venice Beach my whole life. Well, all of the life that counts, anyway."

"I've got no beef with the location. From what Stark said about your skillset..." He trailed off, uncertain how much Damien had actually been authorized to tell him.

"You mean doing covert ops for a top-secret, unacknowledged government agency?"

"Pretty much. You must have made enemies."

She nodded slowly, and though he tried to read her expression, he failed. And when she spoke, she once again surprised him. "You're carrying, right? A Glock 9mm. Right-handed draw. I'm assuming it's out of habit and not because you don't trust me."

He was suddenly aware of the familiar weight. "Habit, yes. How did you—"

"Shoot the window."

He blinked. "Say again?"

She nodded toward the array of windows looking out over the back yard, then reached beside her and pulled out a drawer. She tossed something small at him. He caught it in one hand. "Go ahead. Shoot."

He opened his hand. Ear plugs. She was

either insane or trying to prove a point. Either way, he wasn't inclined to argue. He put in the ear protection, pulled his weapon, and then, after one last curious glance toward Emma, he aimed at the center pane, fired, and immediately cringed in expectation of both the clatter of shattering glass and the flying shards that might— maybe—make it back to where he sat at the island.

But none of that happened.

Instead, the bullet just stopped. From his perspective, looking at it from yards away through the almost obsessively clean glass, it looked like a bullet suspended in midair.

He glanced toward Emma, who looked ridiculously pleased with herself. "Take a look," she offered, but he was already on his way. Sure enough, the bullet had been captured in what appeared to be a one-inch thick pane of glass. And there wasn't even a hint of a spiderweb crack, much less outright shattering.

"What kind of sorcery is this?" he asked, turning toward her.

"We call it science these days." She hopped off the counter and moved to join him at the window. "Lots of R&D where I used to work. I've added a few perks to this place over the years. The scanning system caught your weapon and sent me a text. If you try to pick a lock or pry open a window, you get a nasty shock. And if you were to try and shoot the lock instead, well, that gets really fun. Want to see?"

He balked. "You want me shoot your lock?"

"Nah. I'll just show you what would happen. I can do it manually. But it's automated under certain circumstances." She tapped her phone, and he immediately wished he hadn't taken out his ear plugs. At the same time that metal gates crashed down from the ceiling to the floor over every window and door, a piercing shriek of an alarm started blaring.

It stopped almost as soon as it started, and the fortress unraveled itself, transforming the house from a kickass safe room back into a cute beach bungalow.

"Holy shit," he said. "Do you have a price on your head?"

"Not anymore," she said with a casual shrug. "But you never know, do you? That's just the basics, by the way. There are more bells and whistles." She smiled and batted her eyes. "Don't cross me, okay?"

He laughed, even though he wasn't entirely sure she was kidding. "Wouldn't dream of it. And honestly, I know you're predisposed to tell me to fuck off, but after seeing all of that, I want you on that island with me more than ever."

She glanced around the room, as if the security system were still fully engaged. "High tech security systems get you hard?"

No, but I think you could.

Fortunately, he stopped himself before that admission rattled off his tongue. It might be true, but he had a feeling that saying it out loud would be a very bad idea.

Instead, he told her a different truth. "I'm looking for someone who can hold their own. I'm going in blind here. Possibly to meet someone who wants to help me. Possibly to meet someone who wants to kill me. I don't need arm candy. I need a partner. A female, true. But someone with skills and experience."

She picked up her glass and finished off the whiskey in one swallow. A waste, he thought, considering how fine a blend it was. But then she poured a fresh one, picked up the bottle with her other hand, and started toward the living room. "All right," she said as she walked. "Tell me the rest."

He followed, then took a seat on one end of the overstuffed sofa. As soon as she put her glass and the bottle on the coffee table, he tossed back the rest of his drink, then poured a fresh shot. He took a sip, savoring it before swallowing. To her credit, she didn't press. Just sat back, one leg tucked up under her, as she waited for him to continue.

He rolled his shoulders, got comfortable, and decided to tell her the full story. He wasn't a touchy-feely kind of guy. He didn't believe in oversharing, and he'd just as soon get strapped to a rack than suffer an evening of talking about his feelings. But he also knew that people fought better and worked harder if they knew what they were fighting and working for. And they couldn't make smart decisions without knowing all the facts.

Emma was smart—he could see that. And she'd fight hard for something she believed in. He could see that, too. He wanted someone competent on his arm. So now it was his time to fight for what he wanted.

At the moment, he wanted her. And he was more than happy to toss all his ammo into the fight if it meant that at the end of the day he won the battle. "I'm looking for a man," he said simply.

"Is that who you're meeting on the island?"

He shook his head. "No. As far as I know, I'm meeting a woman."

"All right. Back up and give it to me chronologically."

He did. It was easier that way, anyway. He didn't tell his story often, but when he did he started at the beginning. It was familiar. And that meant he could be unemotional. Just a recitation of facts the way he would with any other assignment.

"My dad was a prick. That's about the sum total of it. But he was a smart prick. Sailed through business school—Harvard, of course," he added, trying out his pathetic Boston accent and making her laugh. "He ended up in international trade."

"Is that a euphemism for drugs?"

Tony shook his head. "No. At least not at first. Later, he probably dabbled. There came a point where he thought he was untouchable. That he'd made so much money it gave him carte blanche on the world, morals and ethics and laws be damned."

She was nodding, so he knew she'd met the type.

"He started out small and he cast a wide net. For a while, he lived in Texas and was going back and forth into Mexico on a regular basis. Eventually, he moved to California and did the same thing, and he started narrowing his business to Mexico and Central America. He was importing all sorts of things, from automotive parts to tequila."

"That's not an uncommon story," she said, "especially for his generation."

"Well, trust me. My dad was not a common man. At any rate, at one point he met my mother. She was going to school at UCLA. Her father was a math professor. And her grandfather owned about half of the real estate in Mexico City. Not to mention a cattle ranch outside of town. The family was basically local royalty. And as far as I've been able to tell, they were powerful without being corrupt."

"What was your mom's name?"

"Santos. Lucia Santos."

Her brow furrowed. "The same last name as your dad. That's a coincidence."

For a moment he was confused. "Oh, no. My dad's father was as WASPish as they came. Trust me," he continued, holding up a hand to forestall her question. "Once I finish, you'll know why I decided to use my mom's name."

She nodded, and he continued. "So my grandfather, the professor, died of cancer and my mom moved home to be with her grandfather at the ranch in Mexico. My father followed. They dated, fell in love, got married. At least that's how the story goes. From my perspective, I think my dad was after the estate all along. And he got it. At least, he got it by marrying my mother."

He studied her face, wondering if he'd either lost her or was boring her. But there was no sign she was drifting. On the contrary, she looked rapt.

"Go on," she urged.

"After I was born, we moved to California and dear old dad got richer and meaner. He started running the ranch. He hired someone to start making tequila. Small batches, very high end. There's more, but the bottom line is he got rich. He got powerful. He started getting pissed off when he couldn't get what he wanted when he wanted it. Because what was the point of money and power if they didn't buy him nice things and respect?"

"My father had no money and no power, and

he got pissed off, too. It's not the bank account, it's the man."

Tony nodded, hearing more in her voice than she was saying. "I know. Believe me, I know too many people who could have bought and sold my father a thousand times over, with more kindness and class than that man ever had. It's nothing to do with the bank account. Not really. I'm just trying to paint you a picture of who he was."

She pulled her knees up and hugged them to her chest, her wide eyes on his face as he continued.

"I don't remember being happy as a child except when he was traveling. Then my mother was alive. My uncle would come over then, too, and I adored him. He wasn't really my uncle. Just a family friend. Possibly even my mother's lover. God knows I wouldn't have blamed her. I never knew for certain. All I know is that she was happy when my father was gone. When he was around, she was like a hermit crab scared into its shell."

He drew a breath, watching Emma. Her expression was flat. Emotionless. As if she was trying very hard not to react at all. He remembered what she said about her father, and had a feeling that she understood his story only too well.

"I don't know if my father beat her," he said simply. "But I know he beat me. And one day, I heard the word divorce. I was only seven, but I knew what it meant. Most kids would run and cry hearing a word like that. I felt like someone who'd finally experienced sunshine. And then two days later, that sun was snuffed out."

"What happened?" Her voice was hoarse, barely audible.

"He kidnapped me. Moved us to Mexico. And then—"

"Wait. How? Surely he didn't go to your grandfather's. So how could he set up there?"

"Oh, I forgot to say. My paternal grandfather could track his heritage back to the Mayflower, but my grandmother was Monterrey born and bred. My dad was born in Mexico, because that was the way his mother had wanted it."

"So your dad had dual citizenship."

Tony nodded. "And so he just went into the country with his son and disappeared. At least until my mother committed suicide and her father died not long after. Then, suddenly, he inherited the ranch from his wife—the divorce hadn't gone through yet. And if there were any questions, well, he just paid people not to voice them."

"So you grew up with him? On your mother's family estate?" He could practically hear the shudder in her voice.

"No. My uncle rescued me. It took two years, but he stole me away from my father when I was nine. By then—by then I knew even better what kind of man he was. Brutal. Powerful. Vile. And he surrounded himself with the same."

"So you lived with your uncle?"

He nodded. "Until I was sixteen. That's when The Serpent came."

"The Serpent." Her voice was flat, and she leaned forward, her brow furrowed in what he assumed was confusion.

"A mercenary my father kept on retainer. A man who did his dirty work. That summer, he killed my uncle. Retribution for stealing me from my father. The Serpent beat him and left him for dead. He died of internal injuries with me at his side in the hospital. And with his last breath he told me that my mother hadn't taken her own life. My father had ordered The Serpent to kill her too. Made it look like an accident"

"I'm so, so sorry."

"So am I." He ran his hands over his face, the

three-day growth scratchy in his palms. "I went after him. My father, I mean. Or I planned too. I waited too long pulling together the mission. The intel. I found some mercenaries who took me on. Trained me even though I was still a kid. I wanted to do it right, you see. I wanted to make him suffer."

He watched her as he spoke, looking for a sign of revulsion that he could actually want to hurt his own father. He saw none. On the contrary, he thought he heard hope when she asked, "Did you?"

"No." The word was flat. "Someone got to him first. Blew him away. Chest. Groin. Face. You probably read about it. It was big news in Mexico and LA. Clyde Morgan blown away by an unknown gunman."

Her eyes widened.

"You did hear about it."

"I—no. It's just so coincidental that someone got to him first. What year was that?"

He told her, and she nodded slowly, as if the year really mattered. "I was fifteen then," she said. "That, um, wasn't a good year for me. I wasn't paying much attention to the news."

He studied her. Nothing visible in her expression had changed. But there was something—something intangible. Something different in the air between them. He wondered what horrors she'd suffered, too.

"So you're going to the island to get intel about The Serpent?"

"Right. The man hunted down and tortured my uncle. He murdered my mother. I've been looking for him for more than half my life. It's a personal mission, but one that led to my vocation. I've trained with paramilitary groups all over the world. Been someone else's hired gun more times than I can count. And I joined Deliverance to make a difference. And all those years, I've been hoping to catch another break. Because I never stopped searching for The Serpent."

"And now you've got a lead."

He leaned back, steepling his fingers under his chin. "A possible lead. It's from a dark web contact who may or may not really be a woman. I've been putting out feelers for years. So this might be a lead. It might be nothing. It might be a trap." He spread his hands, then met her eyes. "And that, Emma, is why I'm not interested in a partner who's only decoration. I need someone who can hold their own if this all goes south."

"And yet," she said, leaning back with just a hint of a grin, "it's still a sex island."

"That it is." He flashed his most charming grin. "Guess it's a good thing you're attracted to me."

She raised a brow, but said nothing. Just swirled the whiskey in her glass. Then she tossed back what was left, downing it in one long swallow. "All right," she finally said. "Looks like you've got yourself a partner."

CHAPTER FIVE

I know he'd expected sex. Of course he did. If for no other reason than we probably should practice before we arrived at the island. After all, we're both professionals. And that means always being prepared. Knowing your weaknesses and your assets.

In this case, I guess that means getting familiar with his ass, among other things. And considering the way he wore those jeans, this shouldn't be an unpleasant assignment.

But, sadly, there'll be no prep work tonight. Not that kind, anyway. I need to make my own arrangements. And since our plane for the island departs at eleven o'clock tomorrow morning, I've only got so many hours left to work.

So I sent him home. And if that leaves him as

antsy and unsatisfied as it does me ... well, he's a big boy. I'm sure he can take care of that himself.

I watch through the window, and as soon as his taillights disappear around the corner, I head back to the kitchen. There's a false panel on the front of the dishwasher, the combination for which is derived by tapping the control buttons in a particular order. I do that now, and the false front unlocks. I pull it down, revealing a standard combination lock on the hidden interior door. I enter that, turn the handle, and open the door to reveal the shallow enclosed space that houses one of my alternate IDs, complete with passport, credit cards, Nebraska driver's license, cash, and a burner phone. I've never been to Nebraska, but it seemed like a good choice at the time.

It's the phone I need, and I take it out, dial the familiar number, then hang up after three rings.

Then I wait impatiently until he calls me back.

I answer on the first ring. "I need to see you."

"You know we can't break protocol. If anyone figures out we know each other from before..."

"I officially joined your firm this morning. Then I quit. But I think I'm back in now. Honestly, I haven't got a fucking clue." We don't use names over the phone, but he knows well enough the firm is the Stark Security Agency.

There is a long silence, then, "I go away for a short assignment, and everything we agreed to goes to hell."

"This has nothing to do with that. And our old boss approved it," I add, referring to Colonel Seagrave at the SOC. "If you and I supposedly meet for the first time through the firm, then everything gets easier."

Winston Noble, aka Winston Starr, was one of the first recruits to Stark Security based on his stellar track record as a West Texas sheriff and other skills that the good folks in Texas don't know about. As it stands, Winston and I supposedly have only crossed paths since my sister got in tight with the SSA. But once I join, we can build on that past, creating a new friendship to mask the old one.

Because the truth is, there's more on his record than what the SSA knows. But *I* know. For that matter, we both know a lot about each other. And that knowledge ties us to each other. Secrets are their own kind of bond, after all. And they come with their own brand of responsibility.

"Fine," he says. "Good plan. I'll see you at the office."

"Tonight," I press. "Please. You know I wouldn't ask if it wasn't important, but I need to bounce this off someone, and that someone can't be our old boss. Are you in town?"

"Got back home an hour ago. I planned to work out and then go to sleep."

"It's not even ten."

"Some of us aren't vampires. And Leah and I have to meet an informant before dawn tomorrow."

Leah's his current partner at the SSA. "You can get your beauty rest later. Come on, man. I need to talk."

"Fine. Forty-five minutes at the drop site. You're not there on the nose, I'm going home."

"I'll be there," I say, then hang up. That's barely enough time to change and get there, but I'll manage.

I change into a tight leather skirt with a slit to my hip that's there as much for walking as for the fuck-me factor. Then I put on a pink sparkly halter that ties behind my neck and back, leaving most of me visible, but providing a surprising amount of support. I pin my ponytail up and slip on a wig. Long and dark, so that the strands brush my shoulders.

Finally, I put in a pair of hoop earrings, some

plastic bangles, and a pair of teetering-tall pumps. I grab my keys, totter to the car, then get my ass to the drop site. I park in one of the overnight spaces a block away, then walk to the battered newspaper machine that's probably older than I am.

On the dot, I see Winston's vintage Ford pickup turn the corner. He pauses, and I lean into the already open window.

"Wanna fuck?" I ask, smacking some fruity gum I'd popped into my mouth for show.

"Get in the damn car."

I do, and he pulls away.

"I swear, if anybody I know sees me supposedly picking up a hooker..."

"Like that's the worst thing you have to worry about."

He turns to glare at me, that friendly, man-of-the-people face going cold.

I raise my hands in apology. "Sorry. Gallows humor."

"You know, Emma. You are actually one of my favorite people. Which just goes to show you how fucked up I am."

"Funny man."

We drive in silence while he circles a few blocks, then pulls into a dark corner of the

Ralph's grocery store parking lot. I start to say something about how if he's concerned about being noticed, maybe driving Old Blue isn't the best idea, but wisely keep my mouth shut.

"You called this meeting," he says as he kills the engine. "Talk."

"I need advice."

"So you said."

"I killed Cane."

He leans back, his eyes wide with both surprise and congratulations. "I didn't know that was even in the works."

"It happened fast. I got some intel on his location. You were gone, so I had to finagle different back up."

"Not Eliza."

"Are you insane? No." Eliza has no part in my work. I've spent my whole life protecting her from that, and the only time she's come close— when I'd gone on the run and she'd tried to find me—both she and Quince almost got killed.

"Who?"

"Quince," I admit, and he groans.

"Water under the bridge," I say, "and not the current problem."

"You need to clean this up, right? In case you get caught. And now you want me to go with you to Seagrave and argue your case for a retroactive kill order."

I shake my head. "No. It was sanctioned. Cane's been laundering money for a bunch of folks that the intelligence community has had its eye on. So in exchange for me getting that information to them, Seagrave cleared it. I don't think local authorities would ever trace the kill back to me—or to Quince. But even if they do, we're covered."

"Then why are we sitting here?"

"The Serpent," I say. "I've got a bead on him."

"Morgan's right hand man?" Winston leans back, looking as shocked and impressed as I was when Antonio told me his story. Only Winston doesn't have to hide his reaction like I did.

I nod. "Turns out a guy named Antonio Santos is after him, too. And he's tagged me to be his partner on the mission."

"How the hell did that happen?"

I give him the rundown, leaving out no details.

He shakes his head in awe. "Only you would tell Damien Stark to fuck off and wear a bikini."

"That's not exactly what I said." I grimace. Because, of course, that's pretty close.

"So it's a good thing Antonio pushed. You wouldn't have known who his ultimate target was otherwise."

"If this is a lesson not to lose my temper and storm off before knowing all the facts, I don't need it. Lesson learned."

"What do you need?"

"I told you. Advice. I'm going in. I'll have access to The Serpent's location through the informant just like Antonio will. And as soon as we leave the island, I'm going to go take the son-of-a-bitch out. I thought Cane was the last. I'd assumed the Serpent had been killed at the same time Morgan was, or at the very least went so deep I'd never find him. Apparently, I was wrong. I want you to help me convince Seagrave to give me authorization for the kill."

Winston shakes his head. "You can't kill him, Em. You know that. He has too much intel locked away in that head of his."

"That's why I need you to help me make my case. The guy's too dangerous. He needs to be taken out."

"Won't happen, and you know it. It's personal to you, and I get that. But the SOC—hell, every covert organization on the planet—is going to want him alive."

"Then they all have a problem, because Antonio wants him dead. And he's the frontrunner in the chase."

"They're going to want you to feed them the information when he finds out where The Serpent is."

"Screw that. This guy did a hell of a lot more than work for Morgan. He's bumped up against my life more than once, and he's not exactly on your favorite person list either. I want him dead, not in a cage. And certainly not being turned and used."

"Emma..."

"*No.*" I practically spit the word, because everything he is saying is true—but I don't like a single syllable he's spouting. "If Antonio kills him, it's murder. But if I can get orders, then not only do I solve Antonio's problem, I get the satisfaction of taking him out. Help me convince them The Serpent's too risky to try to control. He needs to be dead."

"They won't go for it. For that matter, neither will Antonio. From what you've told me, he'll want the satisfaction, whether the kill is technically murder or not."

"Shit." I start to drag my fingers through my

hair, remember the wig, and stop. "Honestly, I wish I didn't know any of this."

"But you do. And one of the conditions of your discharge from the SOC, was that you'd report anything that came to your attention about an active investigation."

"Yeah, yeah. Blah, blah. I know what I agreed to." I release a heavy sigh. Winston is too much of a damn rule follower. Boded well in his role as sheriff, but right now, it's pissing me off.

"This isn't active, though," I argue, albeit lamely. "The Serpent is a cold case as far as the SOC is concerned. Yeah, they want him. But they're not actively looking. Like me, they figured the odds were he was dead or so deep he'd never surface."

"You're splitting hairs," Winston says. "Just talk to Seagrave, but leave me out of it. The worst he can do is say no."

"If he says no, then I'll have to disobey. Isn't it better to ask forgiveness than permission?"

"Christ, Emma, why am I here if you're not even going to listen?"

"And if The Serpent goes after me and it's self-defense..." My mind is churning with possibilities.

"You're forgetting something," he says, and I

turn to him, my brows rising with my silent query. "You push this, and all of the rest of it may come out. You. Me. Texas. You may be throwing caution to the wind, but I'm not. That past is buried. Do you think I want Stark and Hunter and the rest of them looking at me like that?"

My chest tightens. "You know I don't," I say. "But why does this all have to be so difficult. I'm not a puppet on a string anymore. At least, I'm not supposed to be."

He shrugs. "Some strings can't ever be cut. You know that, Em. Don't play naive," he adds. "It's about as good a look for you as that getup."

CHAPTER SIX

There was an upside to having Damien Stark indebted to you, Tony thought. Stretch limos for one thing.

He hadn't expected it. In fact, he'd intended to simply leave his car at the airport after picking up Emma. But when he'd called Stark last night to let him know that things had worked out with Emma, the man had offered him the use of his personal driver and limo to and from the airport. And that wasn't the kind of thing Tony was inclined to refuse.

Now he was back at Emma's house, and although Tony had intended to go to the door—as if this were a proper date or something—she was out of the bungalow and halfway down the sidewalk before either he or Edward, the driver, had time to even get out of the limo.

She was dressed like a woman heading for a beach vacation. She wore beaded sandals paired with a short denim skirt that hit mid-thigh. That was topped with a T-shirt that revealed a strip of her very toned abdomen. It was decorated with a cartoon cupcake and said *Eat Me*. He smiled, wondering if that was for his benefit.

Her hair was dark brown, and though he much preferred the vibrant red that he guessed was her natural color, he supposed he couldn't fault her for taking a few steps toward altering her appearance.

She carried a duffel that Edward, who had hurried around the car to meet her, took as he opened the door.

"Thank you." She ducked as she got inside, and Tony scooted over to make room for her on the bench seat. Her expression was amused, and he made an effort to remain deadpan, as if this was oh so run-of-the mill for him.

"Would either of you care for a mimosa?" Edward asked.

"Why not?" Emma said. "It will be hours before we reach the resort, and I intend to nap on the plane. We arrive early evening, right?"

He nodded.

"We should be rested. I have a feeling this is the kind of place with a nightlife."

It was a good point. And thinking about it, he had to agree that a cocktail wasn't a bad idea.

A few moments later, Edward had poured them two glasses and secured the pitcher in a receptacle that was part of the console behind them.

"Your idea?" Emma asked when they were alone again.

He almost told her it was, but he shook his head. It wasn't. Unlike most of his friends, Tony was not rolling in money. His father's estate—more accurately, the estate his father had stolen from his mother—had been left to a trust when he died, not Tony. And while his uncle had left him a small house in LA, it had come saddled with a mortgage and a list of needed repairs.

He'd made decent money during his years at Deliverance, but he'd spent most of it in his search for The Serpent. Contrary to what the movies suggested, being in the business of vendettas didn't pay particularly well. And ever since Deliverance had shuttered, he'd been financing his quest with the occasional odd job.

With luck, he was nearing the end of that epic journey.

"Let me guess," she said. "The limo was Stark's idea."

"I think it's a peace offering to you."

"Yeah? Well, I might have overreacted, too." Her eyes flashed with mischief. "Not that I'll turn this down."

"Good. We may as well travel in style."

"Indeed." She held up her glass, and he clicked his against it. Then she took a long sip before moving a bit to get comfortable.

He watched, enjoying her pleasure as she settled back against the supple leather upholstery. After a moment, though, her smile faded and she turned to him. "So, we're cool, right? You're not wondering where you stand, I'm not supposed to apologize, and you're not in anguish from a case of blue balls?"

He kept his face completely blank as he reached behind him to push the button to raise the privacy screen. "Care to explain what you're talking about?"

She glanced forward, then nodded at the screen. "You know damn well what I'm talking about. You were expecting to get laid last night, and I sent you home with your tail between your legs."

He sipped his mimosa as he considered his reply. "First of all, my tail was not between my legs. Second of all, yeah, considering where we're heading and the fact that this game needs to look real, I don't think my expectation was unreasonable. And," he added, tugging on the shirt with its *Eat Me* message, "you don't think so, either."

"No, you're right. I don't. Frankly, I think we would have had a blast. That's a plus for the mission, don't you think? At the very least, we won't have to play Go Fish during our down time."

"Depends on what we're fishing for," he said, with just the hint of a leer.

As he hoped, she laughed. "Yeah, well, I am sorry. I had some shit happen last night and I needed to deal with it. Thus, the brush off."

"You didn't get a call. Did a text come in?" He hadn't noticed, but he'd been relaxed with her. His guard surprisingly down considering he didn't yet know her that well. It's possible she'd glanced at her phone, and he'd missed it.

"Yeah," she said, and though it was probably only paranoia, he had the strangest feeling that she was lying.

"So what happened?"

She dragged her fingers through her hair, lifting it, then letting it fall around her shoulders. It shouldn't have hit him so hard, but damn, that move was sexy. "You really don't want to get drawn into my bullshit," she said.

"If we're working together, I think it's inevitable. But if you'd rather talk about politics or religion, then go for it."

"Funny."

"Not really, but it was the best I could come up with on the spur of the moment."

"Well, since you tried so hard..." She shifted on the bench seat, until she could face him better, then reached behind her to take the mimosa she'd secured in a holder on the door. "I had a disagreement with a former partner last night. Some intel came in. I went to take care of it. He says I should let it go."

She finished off the glass, then held it out to him for a refill.

"That's all of it," she said. "Sorry I kicked you out yesterday for such a thin reason. And I'm sorry it's weighing me down today. You didn't sign up to work with an emotional amateur."

"So the intel's related to a cold case?"

"Something like that."

"And he was okay with not acting on the intel?"

She tilted her head back and forth, frowning slightly as if she was weighing options. "Yeah. I suppose that's a fair way of putting it."

"Huh."

Her brow furrowed. "Care to elaborate? What exactly does *huh* mean?"

"I'm impressed anyone can let a case go, cold or not. God knows I've never been able to."

"Exactly." She leaned over and closed her hand on his thigh as she looked into his eyes with sincere appreciation. "That was my point to him. He thinks it needs to go away. I'm all for chasing it."

"I don't blame you."

She leaned back a bit, but her hand stayed steady on his thigh. It was warm, and he was hyperaware of the connection between them. Hand. Eyes. And something more. Something intangible.

He had the sense that she was making her mind up about something, but when she spoke, all she said was, "We're a lot alike. You've been chasing The Serpent forever. I've been working this case for what feels like my whole life."

"It's personal to you." It wasn't a question.

She nodded. "As I said—we're a lot alike."

For a moment, she stayed like that. Her touch gentle, her eyes mischievous, and he let his mind roam through all the things that one could do in a limo. Guilt-free roaming, too. After all, he'd be doing some of those things on the island soon enough.

"Emma—"

"Am I your girlfriend or your whore?"

"Excuse me?" She was still looking at his face, still leaning forward, and his mind was so muddled that he legitimately didn't understand the question. "What are you talking about?"

She sat back, breaking the contact. He drew a breath and felt oxygen return to his brain.

"On the island. Are we a couple that picked Debauchery as our vacation destination? Or are you a guy who wanted a wild time, so you paid a girl to join you?"

"Does it matter?"

"It might," she said. "At the very least, we need to have our story straight."

"All right. You decide."

She grinned. "Yeah? In that case you're paying me five-thousand a day to accompany you."

"Nice to know I have that kind of cash.

Why not be my devoted girlfriend?" He had a few ideas about her reasoning—and the truth was, now that she'd raised the question, he would have come down on the side of professional escort as well. It would be interesting to see how similar their rationales were.

"First, we don't know each other that well, and while on any other resort we could fake it with a contrived background story, this place has the potential to get strangely intimate. Better to stick closer to the truth."

"The truth being that we barely know each other."

"Exactly." She finished her mimosa in two long swallows, then held it out for a refill. He topped his off at the same time. He was feeling a buzz—he hadn't bothered with breakfast that morning—but a few hours of sleep on the plane would fix him up.

"Go on."

"Even as wild as these places are, it makes more sense for you to go off with another woman if I'm not your girlfriend or your wife. And you might have to do that with The-Asst."

"Also what I was thinking." Though he hoped not. He'd do what was necessary for the mission, of course. But the only woman he actually wanted to enjoy the resort with was Emma.

It was an interesting realization. The truth was, Tony couldn't think of the last time he'd been seriously attracted to a woman. Sure, he'd met a few here and there who ended up in his bed. But Emma was the first one he actively wanted to be there for more than just lust or boredom. Not that there wasn't some lust involved. Mostly it was fascination. She'd caught his attention when she'd accompanied Quince onto the tennis court. And she'd gotten under his skin the moment she told off Damien Stark.

There was something about her. A vibrancy. A competence. He wanted to touch it. To hold it. To possess it. So, yeah. He wanted her in bed.

He'd been enjoying the delusion that she wanted him, too. But now that she was mentioning the possibility that he'd leave her to go off with his contact, he had to wonder if he'd misread her entirely.

"Is that what you're hoping?" As soon as the question was out, he wanted to call it back. He sounded like a needy teenager, and he had only the alcohol and his libido to blame.

"What? That you'll leave me to soak up rays in a lounge chair while you go fuck all of this informant's secrets out of her? No, Tony, that's not what I want."

He noticed the use of his nickname, but didn't correct her. He liked the way it sounded. He also liked her answer.

"Isn't it?"

"No," she said, then slid off the bench seat and knelt in front of him, her hands on his knees.

He tried not to react, but he was certain she could see the bulge in his jeans. "Then what do you want?"

"That's not the question," she said, her voice low and sultry as she slid her hands up to mid-thigh. "You're supposed to ask if there are any more reasons for me to be your paid escort and not your girlfriend."

"All right. Are there?"

She urged his legs apart, then scooted in between his knees. Next, she rose up so that she could lean forward and whisper in his ear. As she did, the fingertips of her right hand lightly brushed his cock. It took a Herculean effort, but he managed not to groan.

"There's one more reason," she whispered. "It's because if you're paying me, then you can demand anything you want. And we have to keep up the fiction. So use me however you want. Soft, hard, wicked, dirty. It's up to you. You have all the control."

He swallowed. "Is that so?"

"Mmm-hmm."

"And that's the way you want to play this?"

"It is."

The answer surprised him. From what he'd seen, he wouldn't have guessed that Emma was submissive. Then again, what was that saying? You never really knew someone until you saw them naked. "Why?"

She sat back on her knees, her expression shifting from sultry temptation to all business. "Beyond the simple fact that it fits our roles?"

"Beyond that, yes."

Her mouth curved into an enigmatic grin. "I have my reasons. But don't worry, I promise I can handle it. I spent a significant chunk of my life playing hooker. Even earned a living that way for awhile."

He studied her face, and didn't think she was lying. More than that, he didn't think she meant as an undercover assignment.

"Unless you have objections?" She leaned back, and he wondered what she saw in his expression. "I can be your innocent girlfriend if you'd rather. And you brought me to the island to see if I had a wild side."

He shook his head. "No. No, it's a good plan. The right plan. No objections." The cover did make the most sense. But at the same time, he had a feeling this conversation was about more than sex. That it would impact their entire part-nership on this mission. And yet he couldn't deny that the idea of having this strong, beautiful woman at his command was heady. And, like she'd said, it made sense for the mission.

"No," he repeated. "No objections at all."

CHAPTER SEVEN

"We're so glad you'll all be joining us for a little Debauchery at Debauchery!" The pretty flight attendant for the chartered flight, who looked about as clean cut as a high school yearbook editor and not at all what Tony expected, stood at the front of the cabin now that they'd reached cruising altitude.

"We'll be landing on the island at about six local time, and you should have your room key by seven. That gives you plenty of time to rest, grab a bite, and then join the evening fun by the pool —or just enjoy yourself in your room. That's the beauty of Debauchery—you make your own pleasure plan. Just remember that your concierge is always there to help with anything you need."

Beside him, Emma mouthed, *Pleasure plan,*

then winked. He grinned back. It was a real mission, a serious mission. But at least part of it was going to be fun.

The attendant moved to a console, then dimmed the lights. It wasn't even noon yet, but they were heading to a sex resort with hours of flying time ahead of them. The movie selection on their in-seat consoles was all porn, ranging from soft and sexy to hard-core. And a screen at the front of the plane was showing silent video from the resort itself. Couples and groups naked in hot-tubs. Scantily clad women lounging on recliners. Couples entering private poolside cabanas—and other couples staying outside on the double bed-size loungers. There were scenes in the nightclub. Dancing. Touching. All intimate. All provocative.

Tony knew from the club's promotional material that there were hard-core areas of the resort, too, used mostly by the regulars or very ambitious newcomers. Orgy rooms and BDSM dungeons. None of that was in the video, though. It was all slow and sensual and full of island heat, presumably to relieve the nerves of any newcomers on the plane and get them in the mood to join the party the moment the plane touched down.

He had to admit, it was working. He was already a little drunk, a lot hard, and not regretting this mission in the least.

He shifted in his seat as he glanced at Emma. The seats they occupied were like any airline seats, but the armrest between them defaulted to up, so that it was as if they were on a tiny sofa. They'd reached cruising altitude about fifteen minutes ago, and the tray in front of Emma was down, holding both their drinks. Not that he needed another. They'd finished off the entire pitcher of mimosas in the limo, and he'd already had a nice little buzz when they walked down the jetway.

Still, he hadn't turned down the champagne that the attendant had offered him. What would be the point? It wasn't as if he was driving. On the contrary, he was sitting in a small plane with fifteen other couples, several of whom had unbuckled and, from the intimate sounds drifting up from the back of the cabin, were already initiating themselves into the mile-high club.

Yeah, that refill on his drink was a good thing.

His attention drifted to Emma's bare legs. The skirt was even shorter when she was sitting, something he'd noted in the limo, but had done nothing about. Now, with the sounds of sex rising around them as inhibitions lowered along with the lights, he wanted to touch her. No, not wanted. Right then, it felt like he *had* to touch her.

He told himself that it was the alcohol driving his lust. Either that or the need to seem confident in this woman's body by the time they reached the resort.

Both of those excuses were true, yet neither was the full truth. There was something compelling about Emma. Something he wasn't prepared to examine too closely. Not just yet.

Her skin, though...

That he would happily examine. As she closed the brochure and shut her eyes, he reached over and trailed his fingertip lightly over the skin right at the hemline of her skirt. He waited for her to open her eyes and look at him, but she didn't. She did, however, smile as she uncrossed her legs, spreading them just enough to part her thighs.

His body warmed, and he eased his hand up higher, pushing the skirt as he went until he could see the crotch of her pale pink panties. "Take them off," he whispered.

Her eyes opened into slits. "You want them off, you take them off."

He raised a brow. "Disobeying me? At the rates I'm paying, I expect complete obedience."

For a moment, she only stared, then she very slowly dragged her teeth over her lower lip. "Of course, sir," she said, in the kind of voice meant to make a man hard. It worked. And, interestingly, he also noticed the press of her now-tight nipples against the cupcake T-shirt.

She lifted her ass a few inches out of the seat, then eased up the skirt, fully revealing the tiny silk panties. His breath hitched, and he felt his heart stutter in his chest as those cool eyes looked at him with unusual heat.

And then she slowly wiggled her hips as she eased her panties down, giving him a view of her pale skin and pussy, smooth except for a narrow landing strip. She lifted a brow, then handed them to him. The silk was warm from contact with her body, and he bunched them in his hand, lifted them to his nose, and breathed in the scent of her arousal. "You're turned on."

"Aren't I supposed to be?"

"You are," he admitted. "The question is, what should I do about it?"

She cocked her head, then spread her legs wider. "I'm sure you'll think of something. Sir."

Oh, holy fuck. He might be the one supposedly doling out the cash and running the show, but Emma had his cock wrapped right around her little finger.

"Are you wearing a bra?" He could tell by looking that she wasn't, but he wanted to hear her say it.

"No."

"I can tell. Your nipples are hard. I can see them against that shirt. Is that what you want? For me to eat you?"

She moaned softly. "I think that would be just fine."

"Be good, and we'll see." He traced his fingertip back and forth along her inner thigh, never coming closer than three inches to her pussy. He watched in the dim light. Seeing her body respond. Knowing she was getting wetter, hotter.

Slowly, he trailed his fingertip along the crease between her thigh and her torso, his other hand stroking his cock, hard inside his jeans. She bit her lip and made the kind of whimpering sound that he wouldn't have expected from a woman with the kind of hardened resume that Emma had.

The dichotomy of exceptional operative and needy woman made him want to sink inside her.

To own her. It would be so easy. Just tug her onto his lap. Watch her eyes as she rode him.

Christ, he wanted that. But not yet, he told himself. Not just yet.

Instead, he wanted to make her melt. He wanted to take her to the edge.

He wanted her to beg, and not only because he knew that in the end the anticipation would make the pleasure that much more intense for her, but because he wanted the satisfaction of knowing that he could. She'd put herself in his hands. He intended to make very, very clear that she'd made the absolute right decision.

"Slide your hands under your shirt," he ordered. "Close your eyes and play with your nipples."

"Tony—"

"Did I say you could talk?"

She hesitated, but she complied. Her neck arched back, her hands disappeared under that goofy cupcake. And, oh yes, she spread her legs wider without him even having to ask.

"Now that is a very pretty picture," he said, then sucked on his finger, getting it wet before lightly teasing her vulva, first stroking her labia, then listening to her suck in a sharp breath as he brushed lightly over the hard nub of her clit. She was swollen and ready and it took all of his willpower not to chuck whatever loose plans were in his head and fuck her right there. Why the hell not? Everyone else in the plane seemed to be.

Except this wasn't about instant gratification. This was about—

Honestly, he wasn't sure what this was about other than pleasure. Her pleasure. And his. Because watching her melt was giving him a sense of satisfaction he hadn't experienced in a long time. Probably because he'd never let himself get close to anyone. For him, sex was usually about nothing more than taking the edge off a hard day.

Right now, it was about her. Making her feel. And, honestly, for no real reason other than that he wanted to. Getting comfortable with each other for the island was just an excuse. A good one, but it was as much a cover as their fake names.

No, he wanted this. And the fact that she so obviously did, too, affected him in ways that were both unfamiliar and yet very, very satisfying.

Beside him, she made a soft noise as he slowly cupped her sex, then curled two fingers and slipped them inside her. "Stay still," he ordered when she started to rock against his hand. "This is just a taste," he whispered, withdrawing his fingers so he could tease her clit as he watched her squeeze her nipples beneath the shirt, her muscles tight, her mouth open.

He teased her a bit more, taking her to the edge, reveling in the power he held over her. Such an incredible woman, and yet she was melting under his touch. Dear God, he liked that. Hell, he liked it more than he thought he would.

Most of all, he liked knowing that for this mission—*his* mission—he was the one in charge. Not only of the mission. But of her.

She was panting now, little moans emerging from her throat.

He slipped his fingers back inside her and felt her core tighten around him. And then, because that was the game, he withdrew completely. "You did good," he said. "I'm definitely getting my money's worth."

She made a whimpering sound, then opened her eyes as he took her brochure and started flipping through it. "We should probably be familiar with the resort's itinerary," he said, keeping his voice casual.

She swallowed, her hands still in her shirt.

"Hands down," he ordered, and watched with satisfaction as she reluctantly obeyed.

"Bastard," she said, but there wasn't any heat.

"That's *Sir Bastard*," he corrected.

She turned her head, eyeing him as she adjusted her skirt so that it once again covered her, albeit without underwear. "I can already tell that I'm going to enjoy our mission. But I want to make one thing clear." She leaned over and cupped his cock as she whispered in his ear. "In this game, you don't win unless you make me come."

He shook his head, gently pushing her away as he purposefully turned back to the brochure. "On the contrary, sweetheart. I win when I make you beg."

CHAPTER EIGHT

With the kind of work I do, I've seen a lot of the world. Stunning places like Paris and Sydney and Moscow. And dicey, scary places like underground tunnels where enslaved women forced to work in their underwear put together packages of drugs for cartels.

I've pretended to be a showgirl to take down a mafia-type with a bad habit of killing pretty girls. And I worked undercover at an island in the Seychelles as part of a money-laundering sting operation.

In other words, not much surprises me anymore. But I've never once walked into a resort and been handed a bag of sex toys instead of a room key.

To Debauchery's credit, the toys are very high end. There's also tanning oil, his and hers souvenir towels, a few card games with sensual themes, snack packs of nuts, emergency breath freshener, and condoms.

The goody bag also includes plastic wine glasses with the resort's logo, perfect for poolside. Where, we're told, there are serving stations set up for beer, wine, sangria, and harder drinks if that's your pleasure.

"Meals are served in your room or in the restaurant, and there's always fresh fruit and chilled seafood poolside." Mindy, our personal concierge smiles at us. Not only does she look like a Mindy, but with her perky attitude and equally perky body, she fits in perfectly at this lush resort carved out of the island's vivid greenery.

From what we were told on the shuttle ride over, the island has never had an indigenous human population, but I can't believe Mindy the Concierge ever lived anywhere else. I think she must have been like Aphrodite, rising from the sea in her bikini top and tied-at-the-hip sarong, under which it is very clear she wears nothing.

Keeping with the theme, I suppose.

And, to be honest, I can't complain.

According to Antonio, his contact isn't scheduled to meet him until the day after tomorrow. Which means we may have more than twenty-four hours to explore this place.

On a normal mission, I'd be irritated by the excessive downtime. But right now?

Well, the truth is that I could use a vacation. For that matter, I could use sex. It's been a while. And I'd be lying if I didn't admit—at least to myself—that the idea of sex with Tony is not only appealing, but I'm downright craving it. I liked the way he teased me on the flight. The way he took control. And the way he left me wanting more.

At the moment, what I want most of all is for Mindy to wrap up the pep talk and tour. She's already led us through the interior of the main building, showing us the entrance to the dungeon, as well as the door to the outdoor walkway that leads to the nightclub, the restaurants, the indoor bar, and the fitness center.

All the guest rooms are cabanas, which allows for more privacy. And for quieter surroundings. Especially since this is the kind of place where shouting and moaning and headboards crashing against the wall is expected.

We're heading toward our cabana now, with

Mindy leading us through one of the many outdoor recreation areas. The area is green and welcoming, with spas surrounded by both high and low plants, to provide minimum or maximum privacy depending on the level of exhibitionism of the guests in the water.

As we walk past a spa with low-lying ground cover, Tony takes my hand. When I glance toward him, he tilts his head to indicate the small, steaming pool. Immediately, I feel my breasts tighten as I watch a completely nude woman arch back in ecstasy from her perch on the stone coping. A man in the water up to the waist is bent over, his head between her legs as another man bends over the first, his hands busy beneath the water, clearly stroking the first man's cock.

Tony loosens his grip on my hand enough so that he can brush my palm with his finger, and it's all I can do to keep my knees from going weak from the anticipation of being alone with him.

"There's a lagoon-style pool on the other side of the building," Mindy tells us. "And dancing on the deck at night if you prefer an outdoor environment rather than the nightclub. The nightclub requires clothes, but that pool never does. And if you prefer ocean water, there's a path to the right that leads to the beach."

She pauses, presumably for us to nod and
look interested, which we do. Then she ratchets
up the smile again and continues talking and
walking. "During the day, we offer a variety of
classes—everything from yoga to SCUBA to sail-
ing. At night, we light the torches on the
perimeter of the area and anything goes. You can
check out beach towels from guest services. And,
of course, there is always a staff member nearby
to bring you whatever you might need. From
condoms to cocktails, just say the word."

She flashes a toothy smile, as if she'd just
rattled off the island's slogan. For all I know,
maybe she did.

"Let's see," she continues, obviously running
through a checklist in her head. "If you take that
path to the right, you can follow the trail around
the perimeter of the island. Be sure not to go past
the barrier. We wouldn't want to lose you in the
jungle."

We laugh in appreciation of her little joke as
she nods toward a more civilized-looking path.
"This way takes us to Wanton. That's the section
of the resort where your cabana is. A great location. Very secluded."

We walk a few more feet, then pass a pool
with a sandy, beach-style entrance. Several

women are sunbathing nude, and when I glance at Tony, I can see he's noticed, too. I feel a slight tug of annoyance, and tell myself it's not jealousy.

"Do most of the guests mingle with the people they came with?" Tony asks, and I have to fight that tug again, even though I know he's asking the question in order to suss out how best to find his contact.

"Oh, no. At Debauchery, everyone has the opportunity to get to know any other willing guest in an intimate way."

I glance up at Tony with what I hope looks like lust in my eyes. He reaches out and squeezes my hand, helping me put on the proper show.

"This is our first time at any resort like this," he says. "If we wanted to get to know somebody, how would we go about that? Are there events? Any sort of organized mingling? To be honest, we're both a little shy. The idea of going up to someone in the pool and inviting them back to our cabana is a little overwhelming."

"I hope we don't sound like total amateur newbies," I say, then try out a silly, girlish giggle. Honestly, I'm not sure I pulled it off.

We aren't actually trying to hook up with

another couple. Or with anyone for that matter. Instead, we're trying to figure out the most efficient way of finding The-Asst. Because God knows the woman herself didn't bother to set up an organized meet.

After my close-but-no-cigar almost-orgasm, Tony and I had spent over an hour on the plane discussing a plan for locating his contact.

"You really have no protocol in place whatsoever for locating this woman?" I'd asked, after he gave me a detailed rundown of how The-Asst had reached out to him on a dark web message board.

"None."

"Why did she choose Debauchery?"

"Not a clue. She set the date. She disappeared." He grimaces. "That's about the sum of it."

"No solid information and no clear plan for finding your contact, and yet here you are. You know that this could be a trap, right? Hell, it might be a trap that has nothing to do with your past. I'm sure you made enemies working at Deliverance."

He'd flashed a *well, duh* look my direction. "Do you think that didn't occur to me? I told you

I didn't need arm candy. I need a woman who can take care of herself. With brains and skills." His smile was so sincere that it shot right through me, tingling all the way down to my toes. "That's why I brought you."

"Well, that shows some good instincts at least," I said dryly. "But honestly, you're taking one hell of a risk." We both were, but I didn't say the last part.

"It's the first lead I've had in over a year," he'd said. "I can't not follow it."

I'd nodded, but said nothing. What was there to say? I understood completely.

And now here we are in paradise, where we'll either find out if the lead pans out or end up fighting for our lives. With both options equally possible. And that is part of why Antonio Santos is so fascinating to me. The way he simply dove into this mission, even with such a limited amount of information.

I've leapt before, of course. But always in the midst of a mission, when there's a plethora of other facts that you can cling to like a life raft. He's diving in at the beginning—and not only is there no raft, for all he knows, the damn pool is empty. It's ballsy as hell. And exciting, too.

"There must be something you're not telling me," I'd insisted right before we landed. "Something else that brought you here. Some other bullet point on your agenda."

He shook his head. "On the contrary. I've told you more than I tell most people."

I'd studied his face, played back his voice in my mind. And by the time we touched down, I'd believed him.

Which has, frankly, left me with a niggling bit of guilt since I haven't told him the truth about my interest in The Serpent. Then again, what's it to him? He wants me here because of my skills. He never bothered to ask if I had an agenda of my own.

"Kari?" he asks, and I'm so involved in my memories that it takes me a second to recognize my assumed name. He's still himself—it made sense as he was meeting the contact who might search him out by name—but I'm a free agent, and in case anyone decides to check up on me, we both decided I should be anonymous.

"Earth to Kari."

This time I jump, tugged fully from my thoughts as he nods toward Mindy. I flash her an apologetic smile. "So sorry. I saw this incredibly colorful bird and my mind just flew away with it." It's only a little white lie. A tiny redbird is perched in one of the trees to my left. "Could you repeat that last bit?"

"I was just saying that's what we're here for," she chirps, not looking the least bit irritated with me. "We have games and events all designed to help you mix and mingle."

"Any sort of matching services?" Tony takes my hand with a sultry smile. "We don't want to waste time waiting to meet the perfect companion."

"Of course, you don't. And, yes, we're happy to assist with more traditional introductions. Is there someone special? Did you two notice someone as we were walking this way?"

"No—no one yet," I say. "But, well, most people here are couples."

"We'd like to meet a woman traveling on her own," Tony says. "Anyone you have in mind?"

"Claudia's our only single right now. She's been here since Friday, and she's very well settled with another couple now. Of course, that doesn't mean that one of the other women wouldn't be interested. And if you sweeten the deal with a trade or by letting her current companion watch..."

"That's definitely an intriguing thought," Tony says. "But what about the upcoming guests? Any single women arriving in the next few days?"

"What a good question." We've reached our cabana, and she pauses outside the door to concentrate on pulling something up on the electronic tablet she's been carrying. "It looks like we have three single women arriving tomorrow. Thea, Amy, and Tracy Ann."

"Well, we'd love to meet them tomorrow," Tony tells her, pressing a hundred dollar bill into her hand as he takes our keys. "Your help with an introduction would be very appreciated."

"Of course." She nods to the door. "I'll leave you to explore the cabana on your own. Your luggage is already in your room. And if you need anything at all, just dial zero."

She wiggles her fingers, then takes off down the path.

Tony opens the door, then enters, taking my hand and tugging me in behind him. I stumble, not expecting to be drawn in so quickly, then I gasp as he not only slams the door, but pushes me roughly against it.

His hand slides between my legs. He still has my panties from the plane, and I melt against him as his fingers find my bare sex. His lips close over mine, and I open to him, relishing the way his tongue teases me.

He pulls away, his teeth tugging at my bottom lip. I gasp, more turned on than I want to be as I clutch his ass and pull his body closer.

His lips trail kisses across my cheeks until he reaches my ear. "The place is probably bugged. Audio and video."

I nod. The thought had crossed my mind, too. As far as I know, Debauchery is as legit as sex resorts come. But that doesn't mean they aren't taping the clientele and silently blackmailing their guests. Or even offering to split the profit from amateur porn as a side income.

I twine my fingers in his hair and tug his mouth back toward mine. "I know," I murmur. "This isn't my first rodeo." I slide one hand down and cup his cock, now hard inside his jeans.

He groans and attacks my mouth in a kiss that I'm certain is going to leave a bruise. "Do you have any idea how much I want you right now?" His voice is low and right by my ear, meant only for me. "How much I want to fuck you?"

"I know." The words emerge as a needy moan, and I don't even care.

"You fuck me up," he says. "I'm so glad I brought you, but at the same time, you fuck me up."

"Me, too," I confess, shocking myself with the revelation. Not only that it's true, but that I'd said it aloud.

Not that it means anything. It's not as if I was thrusting out my ring finger and demanding a gold band. We click. That's all. And I have a feeling we're about to click a whole hell of a lot more.

I wish he'd hurry up. My body is on fire, and I'm not sure how much more foreplay I can take before I have to fall to the floor and beg. I want him inside me. I want it hard and fast, and then I want slow and easy. I want to feel him inside me tomorrow. I want to be so sore it hurts to walk.

And since I really don't want to wait any more, I tell him exactly that.

"With me," he says, taking my hand and leading me toward the bathroom. He turns the shower on high, checks the temperature, then strips. I do nothing—I'm enjoying the view far too much.

The corner of his mouth twitches. "Waiting for me to undress you?"

"Maybe," I say, then unbutton the skirt. There's not much to be done to get naked. The tee is easy to peel off, and since I'm braless, that's all it takes. And since he still has my panties in a pocket, all I have to do is shimmy out of the skirt to be standing in front of him completely naked.

He tugs me into the multi-jet, walk-in shower, then grabs my ass and pulls me close for another deep kiss. He's rock hard, and his cock presses against my belly as he leans in to whisper, "If they are taping us, I'm buying a copy."

I laugh, then squeal as he spins me around. I thrust my hands out against the slick tile to steady myself as his hands close over my breasts and his lips tease my neck, his beard stubble rough against my skin. His cock is hard against my rear, and I whimper as he slides one hand down to tease my clit.

"Please," I beg, not even certain what exactly I want. "Touch me. Fuck me."

"Soon," he says, spinning me around again and urging my back against the tile as he slowly licks and kisses his way down my body as the spray of the shower warms us.

I gasp as he sucks on my nipple, his fingers

stroking my clit in time with his suckling. "Tony. You win. I'm begging. Just please, please, fuck me now."

He pauses long enough to tilt his head up, his eyes so full of heat I melt even more. "Trust me, sweetheart," he says." You haven't even come close to begging."

CHAPTER NINE

"Is that a promise or a threat?" Emma asked, and Tony wasn't sure if he wanted to laugh or kiss her.

He settled for kissing her. A fast, flirty kiss that soon turned heated and wild. The kind of kiss that shot through him, making his cock hard and his skin burn.

Honestly, he couldn't remember the last time he'd had this much fun during sex.

He slid his hands down her soap-slicked body, cupping her breasts, and then sliding back up to meet her eager mouth. He'd wanted her on this mission because of the skills she'd developed during her years working undercover in the intelligence community. But now, he was seeing a whole new skillset. One that he had never anticipated she'd excel in to such an incredible degree.

The truth was that it had been a long time since he'd felt this comfortable with a woman. She wanted him to make her beg? Well, he was definitely up to the challenge.

He took the handheld showerhead from its hook, then gently rinsed them both off. Then he took her hand and urged her out of the shower, pressing a finger to her lips when she started to ask a question.

The resort's towels were kept on a warming rack, and he wrapped her in one before drying off himself. Then he led her out of the room and to the bed. He'd noticed the straps as they'd walked in. Not your traditional hotel bed embellishment, but this wasn't a traditional place.

"On your stomach," he said. "Arms spread."

She raised a brow, but complied. He waited a moment, enjoying the view. The arch of her spine, the tight curve of her ass. The two dimples at the top of both cheeks. Her legs were long, with well-defined muscles, and he imagined sinking deep inside her, those strong legs wrapped around him as he exploded inside her.

Soon...

Right now, he had something else in mind.

He moved to the headboard, then pulled out the first tie-down. It had a padded cuff, and he attached it to her wrist, tightening it enough so that she couldn't tug her hand free. He repeated the process with her left wrist as she turned her head and watched him through eyes cloudy with lust.

He met those eyes silently, then sat on the edge of the bed and picked through the resort's goody bag until he found a blindfold. He saw the quick flicker of surprise, but she didn't protest when he covered those beautiful eyes. But when he moved lower to spread her legs and bind her ankles, she finally spoke, her voice a whisper. "What are you planning?"

"I thought you were mine to do with what I choose. Isn't that why I'm paying you good money to have you here with me?"

He couldn't see it, but he could imagine her smirk.

"Are you setting limits?" he pressed, as she stayed quiet.

"No." He thought he heard hesitation in her voice. "I just want to be prepared."

He fastened the second cuff around her ankle and moved back up the bed. His weight shifted the mattress, and she turned her head to

face him even though he knew she couldn't
see him.

He reached out and stroked her damp hair.
"I'm not into BDSM if that's what you're asking.
No need to prepare for a whip or a flail or even a
hard spanking." He bent forward and teased the
curve of her ear with his tongue. "I hope that's
not disappointing. And I promise that no matter
what you were hoping for, you'll enjoy what I
have planned. And, yes, you'll beg."

He stood, then eased up the side of the bed
until he was even with her head. He sat again
beside her pillow, then reached out to stroke her
cheek. She made a soft noise, and he felt the
power of it rush through him. That knowledge
that he was giving her pleasure from something
so seemingly small as the brush of skin against
skin.

"Do you have any idea how beautiful you
are? How your skin glows in the light. Do you?"

He expected her to make some sort of shy
noise, pushing off the compliment as so many
women did. Instead, she whispered, "You make
me feel beautiful," and the power that she gave
him with those words cut straight through him,
heating his blood even more than the deepest kiss
would have managed.

He said nothing, but he was certain she could feel his pleasure radiating through his touch. The soft caress of his finger over the curve of her ear. The heat of his palm as he cupped her cheek. The gentle pressure of his fingertip on her mouth, silently urging her to part her lips and draw him in. He slipped one finger past her beautiful lips, then just about lost his shit when she drew him in, sucking with so much pressure that it was as if she'd created a direct conduit from his index finger all the way to his cock.

He closed his eyes, losing himself for a moment in that sterling sensation of desire that set every atom in his body ablaze. And then, when he withdrew his finger and she moaned in protest, he was once again sliced to pieces by the wild need that grew inside him, hot and demanding.

He wanted her—no question about that. But he'd meant what he'd said. This was about her. More than that, it was about making her beg.

With gentle fingers, he pushed her hair to the side, revealing the delicate curve of her neck. She was strong, he knew that, but naked and bound like this she was so damn vulnerable. Even her bone structure seemed frail. She was completely at his mercy, and there was probably no one in the world who understood what that meant more than he did.

The knowledge both humbled him and made him crave her even more. He wanted to take her to the edge and leave her teetering there until she cried out his name when he finally let her go over. He wanted that control, he realized. Not because he wanted to prove that he was stronger than she was, but because he knew that she *was* strong—and yet she was giving herself to him so willingly.

Most of all, he wanted to go slow and let her pleasure build from a tiny pinprick of pleasure until it was something so massive she'd have no choice but to surrender under the power of it.

Slowly—so very slowly—he trailed his fingertip from the base of her neck down her bare spine. She had the most beautiful back. Her skin smooth, her spine straight, and the gentle dip at her waist before sloping up again toward her ass.

He wanted to slide his hands along that soft, glowing skin, not simply tease her with his fingertip. He gave in to the urge when he reached the two dimples on her ass. It was a thing for him— he had to admit that. He'd seen a Bond movie when he was a kid—he had no idea which one now—but the Bond Girl had worn a bikini and those two dimples had fueled his dreams for weeks.

Now he had to taste them, and he bent over and brushed his lips and tongue lightly over both indentations, relishing the way she squirmed as he feasted.

He'd been standing at the side of the bed, but now he moved to the foot. He eased up onto the mattress, then slid his hands along her thighs until his thumbs reached her core. She was so wet, and she made soft moaning noises as her hips moved beneath his hand. She wasn't begging, though. Not yet.

But then again, he wasn't done with her either.

Slowly, he teased his thumb along her slit, relishing how wet she was and fighting the urge to sink his fingers deep inside her. Hell, to take her from behind right then. But this wasn't about a fast, hard fuck. This was about making her feel. About pushing her to a sensual breaking point, and then watching her face as she finally lost all control and shattered in his arms.

So instead of filling her the way he knew she wanted, he only slipped the tip of his thumb inside her. Just enough to tease around the sensitive edge of her vagina. Enough to have her rocking her hips and whimpering.

But still she didn't beg.

She wouldn't, he knew. She'd hold on as long as she possibly could, and the reward—for both of them—would be all the sweeter for it.

He continued his sensual torture, trailing a fingertip along her perineum, sliding back and forth, his finger slick with the feel of her. His body was on fire, and he thought that he could spend days enjoying the way she wiggled her ass and moaned.

But still, she didn't beg.

She was so wet the sheet was soaked, and he wanted so badly to sink inside her but not yet. He'd have that satisfaction soon enough. This moment was about making her ready. Making her beyond ready, really, and as he lightly traced from her core to the sweet flower of her ass, he knew that he was taking her closer and closer to heaven.

"Tony," she murmured, as he gently pressed his wet thumb against her rear.

"Is this okay? Do you want it, or should I stop?"

"No, it's okay. I like it. I'm not begging—I

want to make that perfectly clear—but I like the way you make me feel."

He couldn't see her face, but he could hear the smile. He could also hear the need, in her voice., and it made him hard. He wanted more, too. Wanted to be deep inside her. But he'd told her that he'd make her beg, and that wasn't something he intended to back off of. Not even if that was her plan—to hold out so long that he was the one who broke.

"Devious," he murmured. "That's what you are."

She laughed, and he knew he'd nailed it. "Nothing's changed, sweetheart. I'm going to make you beg."

He kept only his fingertips inside her pussy. Just enough to tease her as he slid the rest of his body down her leg. He brushed his lips over her soft skin, then slowly moved up her body. She was spread wide from the bindings, and he had plenty of room to maneuver, and as he slowly kissed and stroked his way up, she started to wriggle. Her legs brushed his face, her body shifting under his ministrations. Until finally, slowly, he reached her wet pussy once again.

He withdrew his fingers, replacing them with his tongue. He laved her, relishing the taste, the sweetness. He couldn't get enough of her, and he felt his cock harden even more, desperate for its own taste of heaven.

He slid his fingers between her pussy and the mattress, finding the swollen nub of her clit and lightly stroked her there as she bucked in pleasure. But he wanted to see her face, and that meant that he was going to have to let her flip over.

Part of him wanted to keep her the way she was, on her stomach and blindfolded. But that was punishing him too. He wanted to look into her eyes. He wanted to see the building passion there.

Decision made, he moved back down to her body and slowly, very slowly, he unfastened the straps that held her ankles.

"Giving up so soon?"

He chuckled. "Do you want me to?"

"Never," she said. "I want you to keep going and going, and you won't ever stop because I'm never going to beg."

"Yes, you will. Do you know how I know?"

"How?" Her voice was breathy, and he knew that she wanted him to touch her again.

"Because I know you."

She laughed. "Do you? So soon?"

"Yes." He was certain of it. He'd known at the moment he saw her on the tennis court. He knew this woman. But he damn sure intended to know her better.

Right now, though, he wanted to be inside her.

He moved up her body, then loosened the straps at her wrists so that she could flip over. He tightened them once she did, leaving her spread-eagle on the bed with her arms crossed above her head. At the same time, though, he removed her blindfold, because he didn't think he could go a moment longer without seeing her eyes, her expression.

"Are you going to retie my ankles?"

"No," he said. "I want to feel your legs wrapped around me when I fuck you. But I don't intend to do that until..."

"Until I beg? You're going to get blue balls," she said, a tease in her voice.

"A small price to pay."

He got off the bed and looked in the goodie bag that the resort had provided. He hadn't paid too much attention when Mindy had handed it over, but he thought that he had seen—yes, there it was. A small bottle of erotic massage oil, the kind that heated up when rubbed into the skin.

He pulled it out, taking a condom, too, since he certainly intended to need that soon enough, then he climbed back on the bed between her still-spread legs. He put the oil on his hands, then stroked slowly up her thighs, barely brushing her sex before moving up her abdomen higher and higher until he reached her breasts.

She arched up as he massaged them, paying close attention to her nipples, knowing that the heated oil on that sensitive spot would most likely drive her crazy. Then he used his hand to focus on one breast while he closed his mouth over the other, tasting and sucking, his tongue teasing her nipple as she writhed beneath him. Then, when he had his fill of her—would he ever *really* have his fill of her?—he slid off the bed and stripped off his own clothes.

When he returned, he moved higher up her body so that he could claim her mouth with his. His cock was right at her core, teasing her, and she wiggled against him, her body wanting to draw him in. He shifted, pushing himself down the bed a bit so as to reduce the amount of friction she felt.

As he'd expected, she whimpered in disappointment.

"You know how to get me back," he teased.

"No fair."

"I'm pretty sure that all's fair in bed. Is there something in particular you want?" he asked innocently.

She moved her hips her body arching up and her thighs squeezing against his hips. He planted another long kiss on her mouth, then pulled back, sucking hard on her lower lip before kissing his way down her body, all the way down her clit. He licked and sucked until she was bucking against him, her legs wrapped tight around him.

When he stopped teasing her clit with his mouth, she writhed as if silently begging. And, yes, she whimpered.

"It's okay," he said. "You know that if you lose the game, we both win."

"Bastard."

He laughed, then gently blew a thin stream of air on her sex.

"Damn you. *Please.*"

"Are you begging?"

"Dammit, Tony."

"You called me that on the plane," he said. "I meant to tell you then, only my closest friends call me Tony."

"Oh."

He lowered his voice, giving it a sensual edge. "I very much like the way it sounds on your lips."

For a moment she said nothing and then, "Please. Tony, please, please fuck me."

"Sweetheart," he said, "it would be my very great pleasure."

He slid up her, both their bodies slick from the massage oil. Now his cock was right at her core, and he was about to lose his mind from wanting her. At the same time, he wanted to draw it out, to increase her pleasure, but he couldn't wait. She stole his control. And soon he was deep inside her.

Her hips arched up, and her legs gripped him like a vice, as if she could pull him all the way through inside her, deep enough that they would become one. He bucked against her, thrusting in and out, his body tightening with a growing explosion as she thrashed her bound arms and cried his name until finally, *finally*, she shattered beneath him, her body clenching around him and bringing on his own seriously epic supernova of an orgasm

The next thing he knew he was lying by her side breathing hard, unable to remember when he had ever felt so satisfied.

"Untie me," she murmured, and somehow his

fingers and brain cooperated to manage the task. She rolled toward him, then curled up next to him, her eyes closed as she trailed her fingers over his chest. "As far as I'm concerned, there's not a damn thing wrong with the world at this moment."

He chuckled, then pressed a kiss to the top of her head. "I'm flattered."

She shifted enough so that she could tilt her head and meet his eyes. "I admire a man who does what he promises. You definitely made me beg."

"And you let me do whatever I wanted," he countered. Not that she'd had much choice, since she was tied down, but he also knew she'd enjoyed it. "There's something else I want you to do," he told her.

Her brows rose with interest. "Again so soon?"

He chuckled. "I want to hear your reason."

A flicker of confusion crossed her face before her features went hard with understanding. "Reasons?" she asked, though he was certain she understood.

"For playing the submissive," he whispered, bending close and murmuring the words near her ear. "The woman I pay to do whatever I want. In the limo you said you had your reasons beyond the fact that it makes sense for the mission."

She pulled back, and for a moment he thought she wouldn't answer. Then she lifted her shoulder as if it was all just casual. "You never really know what a man is like until he has complete control." She looked hard at his face, as if daring him to challenge her. "That's when he shows his true colors."

He hesitated, then asked, "Who hurt you?"

She swallowed, then pushed him over so that he was lying flat again. She straddled him, her ass teasing his cock back into attention. Slowly she bent forward as if to kiss him, but she pressed her lips to his ear instead. "I'll work with you," she whispered. "I'll help you. I'll even fuck you. But I am not going to lie down on a goddamn therapist's couch with you. You want to tell me your problems, fine. I'll listen. But don't expect me to share. I don't want to, and I don't need to. Understand?"

He cupped her ass, her curves fitting nicely into his palms. Then he turned his own head to whisper. "Understood."

With a gentle motion, he maneuvered her off of him, then reached over to turn on some music. He'd plugged his phone in to charge, and now he connected it to the room's sound system and turned on a playlist of Nina Simone.

"Nice," she said as he turned the volume up loud enough to drown out their whispers.

"I enjoyed having you tied down," he whispered. "At my mercy. I liked it because I know it heightens what you feel. How that pleasure flows through you. That's why some people are into BDSM," he continued, though she hadn't asked. "I get that. But I got enough of pain as a kid. Some people with my background would have turned it around. Owned it, even. They'd find pleasure and release in either that lifestyle or even in just light play."

He swallowed, remembering the beating he'd taken from his father. Remembering walking in on his dad accidentally when he'd been with a woman he'd strapped to a wall, her back bloodied from a whip. And he recalled the time that it hadn't been an accident. The time his father had made Tony, all of eight years old, stand there and watch.

"That's not me," he said simply as she turned her face away from him.

She stayed that way for so long, he almost thought she'd fallen asleep. Then she said, so softly he could barely hear over the music, "I think we had similar childhoods."

He said nothing for awhile, merely stroked the length of her arm. Then he asked, "What did you mean when you said you'd earned a living as a hooker?"

She rolled over, her eyes lit with fire. "Was there anything about those words that were unclear? And no, I'm not going to elaborate. This isn't the part where we exchange life stories. This was sex. Great sex, yes. But just because I spread my legs for you doesn't mean I'm going to share my history. Got it?"

"I do," he said. But that didn't mean he wouldn't try to learn more later.

CHAPTER TEN

Mindy is bright-eyed and perky when we see her the next morning. Since I've only had one cup of coffee, I'm not yet bright-eyed. And I'm very rarely perky.

We pause for chitchat, and Tony asks if the three single women have arrived at the resort yet. Mindy probably thinks that we came to Debauchery with nothing more than a threesome on our minds, but that's the point of this resort, and she's eager to help.

"Actually, Tracy Ann is in her room. Apparently the flight was bumpy and she's taking a nap to ward off nausea."

"Oh, that's too bad," I say. Since we have absolutely nothing to go on about these women, Tony and I had resorted to guesses. And since Tracy Ann's initials are the same as The-Asst, she came in at the top of our list of who we want to meet first.

"But if you'd like to meet Amy," Mindy continues, "I happen to know she's by the south pool." She gestures helpfully to the south side of the resort. "There's a group getting ready to play our famous Dessert Delight game. You should join. It's one of our most popular getting to know you games."

I look at Tony, only to find him looking back at me. "What about Thea?" he asks Mindy. "Is she here yet?"

"She's scheduled to arrive on the evening shuttle," Mindy tells us. "I expect you'll find her at the nightclub tonight. Almost all our evening arrivals visit the nightclub."

She looks between the two of us, and I can't help but feel a bit chastened. Tony and I had arrived in the evening, but we'd foregone the nightclub.

"Tony and I amused ourselves last night." I meet his eyes and feel the burn of connection race all the way up from my toes to my tits. I clear my throat, trying to remember what we were talking about.

"The cabana's great," Tony says, coming to my rescue. "Very well-stocked for fun."

She beams, as if she'd picked out the massage oil and bondage straps personally.

"Can you point us toward the south pool?" I ask, trying to shift us back to the main topic. "We'll head over there to meet Amy."

"I'm sure you're going to love the dessert game," Mindy says, and as she starts to walk away, expecting us to follow, I once again meet Tony's eyes. This time, I mouth, "Dessert Delight game?" He shrugs, but looks as amused as I feel.

We follow Mindy down the winding walkway to the south pool. Even though Tracy Ann is our best guess for Tony's contact, it really could be anyone. So I'm mentally crossing my fingers that Amy acknowledges the clues that Tony intends to drop.

Since The-Asst hadn't established any protocol through the dark web message board, Tony and I worked out a plan last night to work identifying information into conversations. Like, for example, we intend to mention snakes. The actual word *serpent* would be nice, too, but harder to make sound natural.

And, of course, there's bonus points if we can

figure out a way to talk about message boards or the dark web while chatting her up.

Hopefully Amy will take the bait and prove that she's the one. Because the sooner we can get on with the business of obtaining her information about The Serpent, the better.

The pool we arrive at is kidney shaped, with a jacuzzi at one end and a low diving board at the other. It's surrounded by a wide, flagstone deck upon which sits a number of lounge chairs with over-stuffed cushions. Beyond that, there are rows of cabanas that shade wide, comfy-looking loungers. Each cabana has curtains that can be tied back for a breeze or closed for privacy.

The deck on the ocean side of the pool is currently covered with mats and towels. There are five people standing around, all dressed in skimpy swimsuits. I assume that one of them is Amy.

In the other areas, people are swimming and sunbathing in the nude. The sounds of sex come from the closed cabanas. And, frankly, the sounds *and* sights of sex are coming from a few of the open ones as well. Couples. Threesomes. Even a foursome. And I'm not certain if these folks are just exhibitionists or if the open curtains are an invitation to join. Either way, I'm not even remotely interested.

Which, considering I've never met a sexual encounter I didn't like—or, rather, a *consensual* sexual encounter—my complete lack of interest is a bit odd.

I'd normally put it off on the stress and concentration of the job, but on this particular assignment, that excuse doesn't make much sense.

The truth is, it's about Tony. I'm not done with him yet, plain and simple.

I don't see him as a permanent thing, of course. Hell, I don't really see anybody as a permanent thing. But when we're not on the clock, I intend to take full advantage of the fact that I'm sharing a room and a bed with a man with definite skill in the sex department.

I got a taste last night. Now, I'm craving a more robust meal.

Tony takes my hand as Mindy leads us to a woman who looks to be in her mid-forties with short, curly hair that accentuates her high cheekbones and a diamond studded nose ring.

She's wearing a sarong skirt and a bikini top, her skin glistening with sunscreen. She's incredibly tan. Her smile is bright and cheerful as we approach, and Mindy waves a hand to indicate me and Tony.

"Amy, so good to see you! Meet Kari and Tony. These are the two I told you about as we were walking to your cabana." Tony, of course, is using his real first name just in case The-Asst knows who he is. Another attempt to correct for her failure to establish a protocol.

Amy flashes a sunshine bright smile at both of us. "I'm so glad to meet you. It's so odd coming to a place like this for the first time, much less all on my own, but I only recently decided to quit my job and work for myself, and I thought I deserved a treat before I dove in. So here I am."

She shrugs, looking a little embarrassed but even more excited. She also looks completely comfortable in her skin, and while this may be her first time at Debauchery, I doubt that this is her first time playing sex games with strangers.

Then again, maybe she's just the outgoing type.

Mindy leaves us to introduce ourselves to the rest of the group. There's Scott, a burly man in his 30s with a nice smile and the air of a mall cop. He came with the very young and curvy Beth, who unlike me really is a paid escort, and if I'm wrong on that I'll eat my very sheer sarong.

Roy looks like a male version of Beth and probably is. He's accompanying Clara, a brunette with eyes that are too small for her face and a mouth that's too wide. She keeps eyeing Scott, and I get the feeling that she's very much looking forward to whatever part of this game will pair her with him.

All of the introductions are accompanied by hugs and groping and a few very intimate kisses, which I return. So, I notice, does Tony. Though every time I look at him, I find him already looking at me.

Needless to say, this isn't how I usually act at parties, but when in Rome...

The welcome ritual complete, Scott lays down the rules. Apparently, it's called the Dessert Delight game because of fresh strawberries and cans of squirtable whipped cream that top a nearby table.

"We all have a number," Scott tells us, then proceeds to count off from one to seven. As he explains it, persons one to three lay down, each with our own can of whipped cream. While on the ground, we decorate a few key body parts.

The other three stand in line and come to each of us in turn, "eating" their dessert. They can even embellish with the berries if they want to. Once the last person in line has visited every-one, then the first person in line lays down, and the last on the ground stands up. Rinse, lather, repeat.

Obviously, the game becomes more intimate depending upon where one puts the whipped cream. And, of course, the game is played in the nude.

I glance up at the shining sun and wonder about what kind of burn I'll have in the morning. Still, a job's a job, and once I'm assigned number three, I untie my sarong, strip off my bikini, and lie down on the mat, trying to seem nonchalant. As if this is the kind of game I play every week after book club.

In truth, I'm not really nonchalant at all.

I've done many, many things for work and for survival that required me to be naked when I didn't really want to be. But even I'm a little intimidated by the thought of stripping down to play what seems to be nothing more than the equivalent of a high school game of spin the bottle. Honestly, I'm just not that social. I want to do my job. I want to find The-Asst.

And then I want to go back to the room with Tony.

The realization shocks me a bit, and I look up

at where he's standing, trying to read his face. Is he intrigued by this game?

Is he looking forward to licking and touching these strangers? Or is he only looking forward to touching me? Tasting me?

For that matter, is he looking forward to me at all?

I'm more disturbed by the possibility that he's not even thinking about me than I should be, and I can't stop wondering about my reaction to him. Am I losing my edge? Or, more accurately, has he stolen my edge?

I don't know.

The only thing I'm certain of is that I want him.

Beth, already naked even though she's standing, passes out the whipped cream cans to the three of us who are prone. I'm in the middle position. And since I don't know who my first partner will be, I decide to go easy on the whole thing and put whipped cream only on my breasts.

Beside me, Amy draws a line of whipped cream from her pussy all the way up to her cleavage then dabs her finger in the cream and draws a line across her mouth, as if the cream were lipstick.

On my other side, I can see that Scott has put cream nowhere except his very erect cock.

Apparently I'm the only slow starter in this game, which would make my sister laugh.

The four who are standing, Tony, Clara, Beth, and Roy line up. Roy starts with Scott, and I turn my head to watch, hoping a little voyeurism will get me in the mood. It doesn't. Not until I shift my gaze to Tony, who's still waiting in line. And when Roy reaches me, I close my eyes and imagine Tony's touch, his tongue.

I feel him straddle me, then bend over and very carefully lick every bit of whipped cream off my breasts. I keep my eyes closed, not wanting to react, but not being able to help it. The sun is warm, the whipped cream cool, and I can't deny that his tongue feels nice on my sensitive nipples.

But still, I imagine it's Tony.

Beth is next, and I'm feeling a little bolder now. I put a line of whipped cream right under my belly button and then let it trace up to between my breasts. She smiles shyly at me as she kneels down between my legs and then without another word, she puts her tongue on my clit—completely bare of cream—and strokes slowly upward until she actually reaches a patch of skin I'd decorated.

I suck in air, not expecting that intimate a touch. I can't deny that it feels good though, and that Beth is cute. I consider the possibility of inviting her to the cabana with me and Tony, but dismiss it immediately. It's not that I don't think Beth would be fun. I do. But I don't want to share Tony, and I'm not interested in leaving him for an evening to be with somebody else.

Once again, this is not like me. Somehow, this island has befuddled me.

Instead of sliding into debauchery, I seem to be sliding more into cohesiveness.

That makes sense though, right? After all I'm here on assignment, not on vacation.

Beth lifts her head and smiles at me, the kind of smile that suggests she'd like to meet privately after this get-to-know-you game is over. I manage a non-committal smile back and close my eyes as if in ecstasy as she follows the line of cream up my belly. When it's all gone, she whispers her cabin number in my ear and tells me that she and Scott would be very happy for me to drop by at any time. I make another noise that could be acquiescence, and then it's Tony's turn.

This time I'm more enthusiastic with the

cream. I put a thick layer on my clit that will undoubtedly require a significant amount of licking to get it off. Then I trail it up my belly and dab it on my breasts and beside both ears, giving him a way to whisper to me without being obvious. I'm hoping he had a chance to whisper to Amy—and I want to know what she whispered back.

My knees are up when Tony approaches, and he puts his hands on them as he kneels between my legs, gently pushing them apart. Because of all the cream, I'm less exposed to him than I was to the others, and yet this feels the most intimate of all. It's because I want it. Want *him*.

And I know that I should be concerned about the information he may have gathered from Amy, but right now all I want is for him to bend over and have his dessert.

Fortunately for me, he seems to want it too. He holds my legs apart, and I feel the stretching in my thighs as he bends forward, his breath hot on my skin, as hot as the sun that's beating down on us.

The whipped cream is getting melty, and as he licks it up, I squirm under his touch, wanting more. And when he slides two fingers into me, the first of the group to have been so bold, I arch up and gasp and bite my lip to keep from begging him to do even more than that.

He continues to lick me clean, holding my hips to keep me from squirming. Then he slides his body up, sucking the cream off both my breasts before letting his weight bear down on me, his erection pressing against me as his mouth trails over my cheek to lick up the extra cream by my ear.

"It's not her," he whispers. "I told her my name, got no reaction. I mentioned snakes, don't even ask me how. Again, I got no reaction. Unless she thinks we're being watched, and is being cautious, I'm going to go out on a limb and say it's not her."

"Yes." I add a moan to my voice and hope that he realizes I'm responding to his comment, and not to any particular thing that he's doing to me at the moment.

Although to be honest, my body *is* responding to what he's doing, which happens to be not much of anything. I'm simply hot, tight, and needy all because of his proximity.

Mentally, I curse. I need to stop this. I need to get my focus back. My edge. I have a reputation in this industry, and it's not the reputation of a little girl who goes to jelly when the cute boy kisses her.

"Your turn," Tony says, and it takes me a second to realize that it is my turn to stand and be the aggressor. But I can't bring myself to do it. I trust Tony's judgment. Amy is not our girl, and I don't want my mouth on Beth or Clara or Amy. I don't want to be intimate with Scott or Roy. I want to find The-Asst, and I want Tony.

Base needs, maybe, but I justify my desire by saying to myself that it's practical. Why waste time on finding a witness when I know damn well there is no witness in this pool of people.

So instead of going to the line, I hold on to Tony's hand before he can lay down on the mat. "Sugar pie, I forgot we signed up for that session in the dungeon." I flash an apologetic smile. "We can't stay any longer."

He looks at me, baffled, and then I see the dawn of understanding on his face.

"I'd completely forgotten." He turns to everybody. "I can't tell you how wonderful it was to meet all of you," he says, his gaze lingering on those of us who had been on the ground. "I'm sure we'll see you around."

He leads me away even before giving them a chance to respond, and we walk quickly down the path. Wouldn't want to be late to the dungeon, after all.

"Are we finding Tracy Ann next?" I ask.

"Not just yet," he says, steering us onto the path that leads to our cabana. For the first time, I notice that he grabbed one of the whipped cream canisters off the table. "First," he says, "I think you need a snack."

CHAPTER ELEVEN

"Well, we knew it probably wasn't Amy," I say, as I lay on top of him, our bodies sticky from whipped cream residue. I'd licked off every bit of cream he'd put on himself, and then I added a few more squirts and had a second helping.

We'd fallen asleep, then awakened hours later for a repeat performance. Now both our bodies and the bedsheets are sticky, and I really couldn't care less.

"Tracy Ann does make the most sense," Tony says. His eyes are closed, but he opens them now and smiles at me, his expression full of sensual satisfaction. "The trouble is we haven't found her yet."

"At least we know she's here. She was in her

room, right? Let's go ask Mindy if she'll give us the room number."

He groans in protest, then takes my shoulders as he rolls us both over. He ends up on top of me, his hands on either side of my shoulders as he lowers himself to kiss me. The kind of kiss that's slow and deep and very possessive. The kind of kiss I've shied away from with past lovers, wanting to keep things light. With Tony, though, I want more, and I wrap my arms around his neck and pull him close, wanting this kiss to never end.

When it finally, inevitably, does, we're both breathing hard. He shifts his weight so that one leg stays hooked over mine as he props himself up on an elbow beside me. "As much as I want to stay right here, I think you're right."

He's fried my brain enough that I have to scroll back in the conversation to figure out what I could be right about. "Oh. You mean about Tracy Ann. The problem with that plan is that we actually have to go find Mindy, and that means getting out of bed."

"And getting dressed."

I pretend to consider that. "Actually, I don't think that we do. But I'm going to opt for clothing just the same."

He grins, then pulls me out of bed and into the shower. Which, of course, means it takes us another forty-five minutes to get out of the cabana after one thing leads to another. But, hey —that's the theme of the island, after all.

We're both in shorts and T-shirts as we walk down the path toward the main building. It's past seven now, and the plan is to grab a light dinner from one of the outdoor takeaway stands, then find Mindy. I'll tell her that we had a terrific time with the dessert game. A surprisingly true statement, especially if you only consider the round of the game played in our room.

Tony will tell her Amy wasn't really our type, but that we had such fun meeting other people that we really want to meet Tracy Ann. Then we'll ask if Mindy could point us in her direction.

We start to take the path that goes directly to the main building, but stop short when we see a man taking nude pictures of his partner. Not wanting to interrupt their photo session, we take the alternative path, intending to circle around the fitness center and the volleyball court and come up to the offices that way.

We've just reached the court, when I notice Scott talking with a dark-haired woman in a baseball cap. I can only see her back, but she's wearing a tiny sun dress that is probably doing double duty as a swimsuit cover-up.

Scott waves to us then says something to the woman who turns around and looks at us. She's younger than me, probably late twenties, and she waves, then mouths a thank you to Scott before hurrying toward us with a wide smile.

"You must be Tony," she says.

He and I glance at each other as he nods. "I am. Who are you?"

"Tracy Ann. And I've been scouring the island looking for you."

My heart does a little leap, and beside me Tony reaches for my hand, then squeezes. We were right. Tracy Ann. TA. The-Asst.

This is the woman who can tell us where The Serpent is. At least, that's what she claims to be able to do. There is still the possibility that her dark web message was a trap. That thought reminds me that we had to come to this island unarmed, as the resort has a strict no-weapons policy that it backs up with a detailed luggage search.

Presumably if we did, then she did, too. But that's not an assumption we can bank on. She chose this island for a reason, after all.

At the moment, though, we're under no

visible threat, and I hold out my hand and offer a friendly smile. "I'm Kari. It's so great to see you here." I glance at Tony, who's silently watching her. The corners of his eyes are crinkled, something I've already learned suggests that he's pondering something.

I clear my throat, then make a motion with my head to indicate Scott and a few other guests within hearing distance. "Don't you think we should go someplace secluded to talk."

"Talk," she says, and giggles. "Yeah. I think that sounds like the best thing to do."

She tells us that she knows of a natural hot spring over by the beach.

"It's not a place Mindy tends to point out to first timers," Tracy Ann tells us when I mention that we didn't know such a spring existed. "There's so many other things to do, and that spring is so secluded. It's almost like a perk for repeat visitors."

"Is that why you chose this island?" Tony asks as we walk the path. "Because you come here often?"

Her smile is as bright as the afternoon sun. "Why wouldn't I choose it? What's not to like about this place?" She pauses on the path, then slowly looks the two of us up and down. "After all, you meet the most interesting people."

I manage a laugh and a forced smile, and Tony does the same. I haven't yet figured this woman out, and I don't think Tony has either. But hopefully everything will become clear once we get far enough away from the bustle of the resort. Right now, she probably doesn't feel comfortable talking about The Serpent and why she reached out to Tony in the first place.

We walk in silence for another five minutes or so, then we move onto an even smaller path before cutting through a swath of greenery that opens up on a hidden lagoon. Rocks surround the sandy area, and there, tucked in among some creeping vines and dense grass, is a natural spring.

Tracy Ann flashes a triumphant smile. "Awesome, right?" she says as she pulls off her dress, leaving her curvy body completely naked. So much for my guess about a swimsuit.

She walks to Tony and starts to unbutton his shorts. "Don't be shy," she chides when he takes a step backward, his eyes darting to me. "Let's get in. Unless you don't want what I'm willing to offer," she adds, glancing at me as if to indicate that I'm invited to this party, too.

"No," Tony says, then clears his throat. "We're, ah, definitely interested."

I watch as he peels off his clothes, already feeling possessive about that magnificent body. His eyes seek out mine, and he subtly cocks his head as his eyes widen in an if-I'm-in-so-are-you kind of way.

Apparently he doesn't intend to play this game by himself. Honestly, I'm glad.

Tracy Ann glances over her shoulder at me, then moves to get into the spa.

I strip and hurry into the water as well. I'm feeling a little too exposed even as I'm chastising myself for acting like a prude. I used to have an edge, and I fear that somehow meeting Tony has dulled it.

As if to prove my own theory wrong, I slide close to Tracy Ann. "You've been looking for us," I say. "Or you've been looking for Tony, anyway."

"Oh, you, too," she says, then brushes her fingertip over my lips as she smiles into my eyes. She has a beautiful body, not too thin, with all sorts of delicious curves. And her other hand is on my thigh. If this were a party a year ago with some casual acquaintances in Santa Monica, I'd be fantasizing about getting lucky tonight.

Come to think of it, that's exactly what I'm

fantasizing about. Only not with Tracy Ann. The only one I want to get lucky with is Tony.

I frown, not sure I'm comfortable with this new me or my so-quick, so-hot reaction to this guy. And as if I can counteract my own confusion, I reach up to catch her finger on my lip, then gently draw it into my mouth.

She makes a little moaning sound, and I close my eyes. And when I do, it's Tony I imagine.

I open them to find him watching me, still standing on dry ground. I detach myself from Tracy Ann and hold out my hand to him.

"I don't know," he says. "Maybe I just want to watch."

"What if I want you in here?"

"What if we both do?" Tracy Ann adds.

Tony's eyes stay on me, and I silently mouth, *Please*.

He nods, his focus on me alone as he gets into the small, natural pool, sighing with pleasure as he sinks into the heated water.

The spot really is luxurious. I'm not sure what I think of Tracy Ann, but she definitely picked a good location to talk. I also know why she arranged to meet on this island. Clearly she comes here often. As a regular, it's a safe bet that the staff looks out for her. She's taking a risk, too, by reaching out to Tony. If she goes missing, the staff would undoubtedly notice—and try to find her and help.

Coming here to this familiar place is one extra level of protection for her.

Tony settles onto the stone ledge near me, and immediately Tracy Ann moves over and straddles him. She shoots me a grin. "Joining or watching?"

Since there is absolutely no fucking way I am watching her screw my partner, I slide over.

"You have a condom?" she asks.

And even though I know he has one of the island-issued condoms in his pocket, he says, "Sadly, no."

"Oh, well," she trills, reaching for his hand and slipping it under the water and between her legs. "We'll have to make do," she murmurs as I steam—and not because of the overly warm water.

He opens his mouth—presumably to say something—but she leans in and captures him in a kiss. Then she breaks it and urges me closer, cupping me around the neck and pulling me in close for a long, slow kiss.

I don't back away. If this is the way to get to know our contact, then so be it. And the truth is,

I don't entirely hate the situation. For one thing, she's a damn good kisser. But what is really turning me on is the way Tony has lifted my other hand and is now sucking on my finger. Hard. So that the sensation goes all the way to my core. A core that he is decidedly *not* touching —and a cold slash of jealousy cuts through me when I remember what he's doing with his other hand.

I break the kiss, pulling away from Tracy Ann to meet Tony's eyes. His hand emerges from the water, sliding up her body to tease her breast. I feel my eyes narrow, and I'm certain he can tell I'm jealous. Strangely, I don't care. Then he smiles, and I feel his other hand on my thigh, and I swear I start to melt. Especially when he reaches around to cup my ass and urge me closer. I comply, and soon he's using that hand to part my thighs, something I help with eagerly. And when I feel his thumb on my clit—when he slips two fingers inside of me—I close my eyes and whimper.

I open them again when I feel the light touch of fingers on my breast. I expect them to be Tony's, but the fingers belong to Tracy Ann, who leans in and claims my mouth. I tense, thinking about Tony, but his fingers thrust more deeply into me, and since this obviously doesn't bother him, I lose myself in the kiss and the incredible sensations that Tony's fingers are sparking in me. And, yes, the thrill of knowing he's enjoying watching.

I reach out my own hand and find his cock, stroking it under the water. We're a tangle of limbs and sensations, and while I like the feelings that are spinning through me, what I like more is the fantasy that it's just me and Tony alone under the darkening sky.

Tracy Ann's fingers twine in my hair, pulling me closer as she deepens the kiss. Tony's fingers are stroking me expertly, but it's not until he puts his hand over mine and stops my motion that I open my eyes. *Only you,* he mouths, and it's as if he's spoken an incantation. Suddenly, waves are breaking over me. I pull away from Tracy Ann, arching back as I reach out for Tony. He takes my hand, then pulls me the short distance across the water and kisses me, long and hard as the last tremors wrack my body.

"Now that could make a girl get jealous," Tracy Ann says.

"I confess I'm not sure of the etiquette. Do I owe you an apology?"

She shakes her head. "Oh, no. You got me

primed for the rest of the night." She shoots a sultry look in my direction. "You both did."

Tony shoots me a wicked grin, then turns back to her. "Maybe now we should talk about The Serpent?"

Tracy Ann's eyebrows raise, then she casts her eyes down. "Is that what you call him? My ex called him Roger. I never understood that."

"No," I say. "Not Tony's assets. The Serpent. Isn't that why you found us?"

Tracy Ann's brow furrows as she slowly shakes her head. "I was looking for you because you were looking for me. Mindy said so."

Tony and I meet each other's eyes, and I honestly can't tell if he wants to laugh or cry.

"I thought maybe we'd met before," Tracy Ann continues, as she gets out of the spring and pulls her dress over her wet, naked body. It clings, mostly see-through in the fading light. "Or that you heard about me from a friend of a friend. So what's the serpent? A new kind of sex toy?"

"Ah, not exactly," Tony says.

"Well, come have a drink with me and tell me all about it."

"Why don't we catch up to you?"

"Sure thing." She winks at us. "Don't have too much fun without me. And don't be offended if I'm having fun with someone else when I see you again. That's what I love the most about this place. It's so easy to meet new people."

"Yeah," I say. "We love being social."

Tracy Ann laughs, wiggles her fingers, then heads off down the path.

Tony pulls me closer, then nuzzles my ear as he whispers, "What the hell was that?"

I laugh as I settle on his lap, feeling his cock rise to the occasion. "As far as I'm concerned, it was foreplay. Take me back to the cabana?"

"Not a chance," he says, shifting so that we both slide off the stone bench and into the water. "I'm going to take you right here."

CHAPTER TWELVE

"Alone at last," he says.

I grin and move closer in order to straddle him. "This is what I wanted," I say. I hook my hands around his neck and pull him close, bending down for a kiss that tastes like salt water. Then I wiggle against him and feel his cock stiffen between my legs, rubbing my pussy in a way that makes me want even more.

"You lied, you know."

"Did I?"

"You told Tracy that you didn't have a condom. I'm going to be very sad if that's true."

"Just trying to conserve resources for where it matters," he says.

"Very glad to hear it." I put my hands on his shoulders, then slowly move them down. I'd been mostly bound last night, and though my hands were free to roam when he'd been gooey with whipped cream, I haven't yet gotten my fill of his body.

Now, I'm going to take full advantage.

He's slick from the water and my hands move easily over him. He closes his eyes as I explore, and I wriggle with pleasure, realizing that he is enjoying being touched as much as I had when he'd had me bound.

I slide my hands lower, trailing below the water line as I run my fingers through the hair on his chest, amusing myself by tracing patterns before moving on to tease his nipples at the same time that I bend close for a kiss that I end by tugging on his lower lip with my teeth as my hand moves further down.

I trace the line of hair from his chest to his abdomen and then all the way down to his cock, now as stiff as a rod.

"This is interesting," I say as I curl my hand around his shaft, then stroke him slowly, keeping up a steady rhythm as he closes his eyes and murmurs, "Oh, sweetheart, yes."

I smile, pleased by his reaction. The sounds of pleasure. The obvious arousal. And, of course, the increased tempo of the pulse in his throat.

I feel powerful. In control. I like it. Of course, there's no doubt that I also like submitting to this man. I think we both proved that last night, but there's something incredibly satisfying about bringing a strong man to his knees.

As if to prove the point, I tighten my fingers around his cock and increase the tempo of my up and down strokes, putting pressure on the vein and teasing the tip with the ball of my thumb with each motion.

"On me, sweetheart," he demands. "Find the damn condom and ride me."

Since that's an invitation I'm not about to ignore, I do what he says. I find the condom that he's fumbled from the pocket of his discarded pants. I manage to open it with one hand and my teeth, and then I release his cock long enough to sheath him.

I straddle him, rubbing the tip of his hard cock against my core, teasing myself and him before finally impaling myself on him in one powerful downward thrust so that we both feel the intensity of this connection.

I bite back a cry as he fills me, and he groans with equal intensity, then cries my name so that it echoes around us, making me even more turned on. He cups my ass, then lifts me, maneuvering me up and down as he whispers for me to stroke my clit and his cock at the same time.

I do, and the flurry of sensations is too much, the pressure building too fast, filling me up with so wild intensity that I have to use my free hand to hold onto his shoulder to keep me from flying out into space.

He uses one hand to hold my head steady as he kisses me hard and deep with teeth and tongue, the intensity of the kiss mimicking our fucking, and it's almost too much. I'm over-whelmed by sensations, and yet I want more. I want it all. All of Tony. Everything he's willing to give.

It's intense. Scary even, and yet I already cherish this connection. I already fear what will happen when we leave this island, because I don't want this to end. I don't want *us* to end.

"Do you have any idea how beautiful you are right now. Your body flushed, your mouth open. You're so close to coming, all I want to do is watch you."

His words tease me in delicious ways. He makes me feel beautiful, and I moan as my body tightens. I feel my pussy clench hard around him as I'll never let go, as if my body is trying to time it so that we come together, as if it's absolutely imperative that we do.

"Please," I beg.

"Please what?"

But I can't answer that because I don't know. All I can think of is everything. And as I get closer and closer and closer to that inevitable explosion, he closes his mouth over mine in a kiss that is so wild and hard and possessive that I swear I would orgasm even if he wasn't inside me, even if he wasn't playing with my clit, even if this pressure wasn't building and building. Because he's fucking with me with his mouth and his cock and I'm about to go over the edge.

And then, oh God, the world explodes, and I arch back, our bodies still connected, my eyes wide open, as I look at the stars and wonder if I really and truly reached them.

"Wow," I say as I lay back onto the water, his splayed hands keeping me afloat. "We may have to stay here all night. I'm not sure I can move."

"If you can't, I'll carry you."

I manage to lift my head enough to see him in the dark. "You really do have stamina."

He laughs. "For you? I have a never-ending well of energy."

I make a contented noise that shifts to a startled *oh* as he gently pulls me closer, then settles me on his lap. The fingers of one hand are twined in my hair, and he pulls me close, kissing me deeply. "I don't know if it's you or this island, but I can't seem to get my fill of you."

I want to tell him I feel the same, but his words make me feel antsy. As if he's talking about more than sex. As if this thing between us is real and not just part of a lust-filled island mission.

So I push down what I'm actually feeling and instead brush a kiss over his lips as I whisper, "This evening has been very, very hot and very, very strange."

"Has it?" He runs his hands up my body to cup my breasts. "I have no interest in sharing you all of the time, but I'll confess to having a good time. Even if under false pretenses. And I definitely liked the way the evening progressed after Tracy Ann left."

"Me, too," I admit.

"And I liked watching you kiss her. You seemed to like it, too."

I bend forward to whisper in his ear. "I'll tell you a secret — I like pussy, too. Does that bother you?" I've been with guys who were disgusted by the idea of two women together and guys who dreamed of watching, as if the thought of watching me with another woman would be his own personal live-action porn channel. I didn't think Tony had that voyeuristic bent—he seemed an all-in participant. But we're both playing a role on this island, and I realize I'm holding my breath, hoping that he's not freaked out by the fact that I'm bi.

His hands are roaming all over me, as if he can't get enough of the feel of my skin against his. "So long as you like my equipment as well," he says, taking my hand and cupping his cock, "I don't have a problem with that at all."

He's slowly stroking, moving my hand up and down beneath the water. "I like it," I say, my voice heavy with desire all over again, as if I really, truly cannot get my fill of this man.

I whimper, then shift my position, so that instead of straddling both his legs, I'm only straddling one—which means I can grind against his leg in time with the movement of our hands. "I like it very much."

I hook my free arm around his neck, then bend closer to whisper in his ear, surprising myself when I confess, "I didn't like you touching another woman."

"Didn't you?" The surprise in his voice seems genuine. "It didn't turn you on?"

"It did," I admit. "But I still didn't like it. It's just that..."

I trail off. I don't want to voice my jealousy. Jealousy means I'm invested. And I know better than to get invested with a partner on a mission. Or ever, for that matter.

I like Tony. I do. We're ridiculously compatible in bed. He's smart. He's competent. He makes me laugh and God knows he makes me come. But we're at a sex resort. What's not to like? It's not as if we're going to go back to LA and start playing house.

"Are you going to sign on to work for Stark Security?" I hear myself asking.

He frowns, probably confused by my left turn away from the topic of sex. "I'm thinking about it," he admits. "I'm focused on taking down The Serpent. Hell, I've been focused on that for an eternity. And if—no, *when*—I do..." He shrugs, then continues, "Well, a lot of stuff I've been avoiding or putting off opens up."

"Like a real job?"

"Real job. Real life. I've been a nomad. I like the idea of roots."

He looks at me as he says it, and I feel that quickening inside me again. I don't want to fall for him. Friends, family, love — all of that makes you vulnerable. Eliza's already my weak spot. I know that, but I deal with it because she's worth it.

But I'm not sure I can handle another weakness.

At the same time, I'm not sure I have a choice. Because whether I want him to or not, there's no denying that this man is growing on me.

CHAPTER THIRTEEN

"Did I lose you?" Tony asks gently, bringing me back from my thoughts.

I shake my head. "No, no. Sorry." I flash an embarrassed smile. "It's just what you said. Roots can be good, you know. Trust me. I went a long time without having any."

His eyes are warm and full of compassion. "Why? What happened to you when—never mind."

He cuts the question off sharply, and for a moment I don't understand his hesitation. Then I remember I bit his head off when I'd mentioned turning tricks.

"No, it's okay." I draw a breath, then say the most important part. "I don't mind talking about it now." What I don't tell him is that I actively *want* to tell him. I want to know him better. And I want him to know me, too. "Bottom line is that I had a shit childhood, a scary adolescence, and nomadic, semi-solitary adulthood. Then it got better."

That, of course, is the top of the mountain description, and I study his face, trying to see if he really wants to know more. I don't have to guess, though, because he takes my hand. "Tell me," he says. He doesn't ask if I want to talk about it. Doesn't say I can vent to him if I want. Instead, he says, "tell me," in a voice that makes it clear that not only is he curious, but he cares.

"Start with your childhood," he urges. "I have a feeling yours wasn't any better than mine. Honestly, I'm guessing that it was worse."

I feel tears prick my eyes and hope he doesn't notice. I'm not a crier. I've been trained to hold in my emotions, to move past them and focus on the goal. But maybe right now, feeling that emotion should be my goal. Sharing what I went through with someone who understands but isn't Eliza or some government shrink who's analyzing me even as he has me hooked up to a polygraph.

"Hey," he says, moving his arms around my waist. "No pressure. I want to know, but only if you want to tell me."

"I do." I release a weird-sounding laugh. "I think I really do." Another breath, then, "Right. I —I barely remember my mother. I can remember her being pregnant. I was almost seven. I remember her reading to me, holding me, brushing my hair. And I remember coming into her bedroom to find her curled up in a corner, her arms around her belly crying. I only saw him hit her a couple of times, but I think that's why I remember it so clearly, even though I was so little. Because I knew there was a baby inside her, and I was so, so scared that something would happen to my little sister."

I manage a little smile. "I knew it would be a sister. I was so certain, even though Mom didn't know herself. Or maybe she did, but didn't tell my father. He wanted a boy, of course."

"He sounds like a major son-of-a-bitch."

I feel my eyes go hard. "I've apprehended a lot of sick fucks over the years. And I've killed more than my share, too. Everyone was vile and dangerous and I don't regret a single one of those jobs. But not one of them was as pathetic and horrible as my father. Not one."

"I believe you." He moves one hand from my waist, then uses it to stroke my hair as he holds my gaze. "What happened when your sister was born?"

"I remember being happy. She was so sweet and little, and my mom told me that I had to be sure to watch out for her because I was her big sister." I have one hand on his shoulder, but I trail the fingers of my other through the water, watching the ripples. "I didn't think about it at the time, but later, I thought it wasn't just the typical big sister talk. You know, a *don't be jealous because she's yours too* kind of thing."

The sunlight is fast fading, but I can still see the way his face tightens and his throat moves as he swallows. "He killed her."

"Yes." I close my eyes, gather myself, then try again. "He must have, but I don't know for sure. She—she disappeared when Eliza was just a toddler. I don't think she even remembers Mom. But he must have killed her. She wouldn't have just left us to save herself." I look at him hard, as if defying him to argue.

"No. I don't believe she would, either. She had to know how bad it would be for the two of you if she wasn't there as a buffer."

One of the damn tears escapes and trickles down my face, my heart breaking with both the memories and from the simple fact that he gets it. It feels nice, and that's not something I expected.

It feels strange to be talking about my past since I so rarely do this. Why would I? It's horrible and painful and I had to discuss it backwards and forwards to a million different shrinks and commanders after I was recruited into the SOC. I hadn't liked that feeling of being examined and judged. And once I wasn't forced to talk about it, I never did again. Not even to the people I was close with. Not Lorenzo, my partner in the PI firm. Or even Cass, who knows about a lot of it from talking with Eliza, but never got a word of it from me.

But with Tony, it doesn't feel weird or painful to share. Maybe because I know he suffered, too. The loss of his mom. The vile and controlling nature of his dad.

"Do you want to tell me what he did to you?"

I shake my head. "Whatever you're imagining," I say, "it was worse."

"You protected Eliza."

I don't even bother to brush away the tears as I nod. "I had to. I was all she had."

"And you love her."

I nod. Sometimes I forget how much that plays into it. When you grow up the way I did, with only survival on your mind, things like love don't seem to matter. Or maybe they matter so much you don't see them. They're the fabric of your life. The thing that holds it all together. But even then, love doesn't feed you or clothe you or put a roof over your head. Not that I'd seen, any way.

"You got away from him, though," Tony says, obviously figuring out where my story is heading. "How?"

"I killed him," I say bluntly, my eyes on his, waiting to see him cringe. He doesn't even flinch, and I feel my body relax even more.

"How?"

"I pushed him down the stairs. To be honest, we were just trying to escape. Our room was a basement storage closet. No windows. No nothing. But I told Eliza we were getting out, and I pushed him. I wasn't trying to kill him—slowing him down and getting away were all I could really think about—but I was hoping he'd die. After all, death was the only thing that would be sure to work. Where we could be certain he didn't catch us. And," I add, not the least bit ashamed of the confession, "the idea of him living on—just existing after we ran—made me sick to my stomach. I wanted him dead. And after all the times he—" My voice catches. "After everything he did to me from the time I was six until I was fifteen ... well, yeah. I wanted him to die."

"Fucking prick," Tony says. "I hope he suffered, broken and in pain before he went to hell."

A sad smile flickers on my lips. "Yeah, me, too. But I don't know. I never looked back. Never even checked the newspapers. I was fifteen years old and on the run with my little sister. We took a bus to Los Angeles, and we lived on the street."

"At fifteen. Christ." He takes his hand from my hip and runs it though his hair. Immediately, I miss the contact. The connection. "Why didn't you go to a shelter?"

I shake my head. "They might have separated me and Eliza. I learned the truth years later—he died in that basement—but back then I didn't know if he'd survived or not. If he had, he might find us if we were on the grid. If he was dead, someone might find out what I'd done."

He looks so profoundly sad I want to reach out and comfort him, and it warms me to know how much my story is affecting him. After a moment, he says flatly, "You turned tricks so the two of you could stay alive."

There's no judgment. No emotion. He's just stating a fact, and that flat simplicity gives me the strength to tell him the rest. How I prostituted myself so we could have a decent apartment and money for fake IDs, not to mention money to hire someone to pretend to be our parents long enough to get Eliza enrolled in school. Me, I didn't have time for that.

And, yeah, crime does pay. I tell him about that, too. About how I shoplifted. Did whatever I had to do to keep my little sister alive. And I told Eliza all of it.

"All?" His brows rise with the question.

"Yeah," I say. "Granted, the details were tied up with a pretty bow until she was old enough to really understand, but yeah. The whole ball of wax. Turning tricks and all."

He says nothing, but his brow crinkles enough that I feel compelled to continue. With anyone else, I probably would drop it. Hell, with anyone else, I wouldn't be having this conversation. But Tony's different. I want him to understand.

"She was all I had. And I was all she had. We'd grown up in a house filled with lies and pain and the kind of stuff that two kids should never have had to deal with. I wanted her to have total honesty. It's not like I needed to dress up our new life. Even with me working the street, we were better off. Happier. Healthier. She wasn't even ten, but she got that."

"I get it," he says gently. "I just hate that either of you had to experience it."

I shrug, resisting the urge to squirm. I'm not a touchy-feely person. And while I appreciate compassion, I never quite know what to do with it.

"Yeah, well, it got hard to keep the promise later."

"But you did."

I nod. "Yeah. Always."

"What happened later that made it harder?"

I meet his eyes, because it's important I see his reaction. "I killed somebody." My mouth is bone dry, the memory of that horrible day washes back over me. The shock on Eliza's face when the verdict came in. And again when the judge sentenced me. "I got the death penalty. I was eighteen and my lawyer said the judge was making an example of me."

"Good God," he says. "You must have been terrified. Not just about you, but by what would happen to Eliza."

And that's it—that's when I can't hold the

tears back anymore. Because he gets it. I can't quite wrap my head around it, but he really, genuinely gets me.

"What happened?"

The story is long and convoluted, but the bottom line was that if I didn't help with a job, the prick who was blackmailing me would kill Eliza. I helped, and it all went south when someone else on the team killed an innocent woman. I said I was out. The prick said he'd kill my sister. So I took him out.

"And they nailed you for his murder and for the murder of the woman," he guesses after I give him the story in a flat, emotionless voice.

I nod. "And no one could corroborate my story. And it got even worse when the others on the team banded together and pointed the finger at me for both deaths, too. It was bad. I was terrified." I hug myself, remembering that cold fear. Not so much for me, but for Eliza.

"And yet here you are."

I nod. "Do you know Anderson Seagrave? He's a colonel in the SOC."

He shakes his head. "Should I?"

"He knows Stark. I thought maybe your paths had crossed. He was a newbie, then. This was almost twenty years ago. He's my guardian angel. He and his boss pulled me out, and Seagrave became my handler. My record was wiped clean by the government."

"And in exchange, you became theirs. Covert ops."

"Got it in one." I draw a breath. "But it worked for me. I had a solid salary, and for the first time Eliza and I had a clean place to live with food always in the fridge. I got a cover job as a private investigator with an ex-cop who'd helped me and Eliza out here and there after he found us sleeping in a car. Lorenzo. It was part cover, part real. And after I left intelligence, I worked as a PI for real. I just sold him my half of the business. Figured I couldn't really hang on to it once I joined Stark Security."

He looks at me with something like respect, and I melt under his gaze. "I'm so sorry you had to go through that. But it all molded you into an incredible woman."

His eyes are on mine, and for a moment, it feels like time has stopped. Then he reaches up and trails his fingers through my hair. Something has shifted. The heavy, dark reality of my story replaced by something equally intense but tinged with heat and longing. Even respect.

I see his lips part. And though I don't know

what he's about to say, I know that I want to hear it, even though that intense fire in his eyes scares me.

"Emma, when we wrap this up—I mean, when we find The Asst—do you think—*Oh, holy fuck.*"

He stands as says the last words, and the action sends me toppling into the water. I gasp, and he reaches a hand down to help me. But he doesn't look apologetic. Instead, he looks euphoric. "We're idiots," he tells me, and in a heartbeat the mood shifts from something heavy and personal to the calculating reality of our work.

"Tell me," I demand.

"Thea," he says. "It's so fucking obvious."

I shake my head, clueless, then freeze as the light dawns. "Holy shit, you're right. The-A."

He nods. "Thea. The Asst."

I twine my fingers in his hair, then pull him closer for a long, slow kiss. When we break apart, we're both breathing hard. "Rain check," I say. "Now let's go find your contact."

CHAPTER FOURTEEN

When Tony called Thea's room, the resort operator put him through, but after five rings, it flipped back to the operator who refused to give him her room number.

"I understand you think that she wants to see you, sir," she'd said. "But our obligation is to all of our guests, and since we have no way to confirm, we simply can't release the number."

As far as dead ends went, that was pretty rock solid. Which explained why he and Emma were now heading toward the resort's main building. "The odds of her being with someone right now are slim," Emma said. "After all, she's here to find you. Although it's a bit odd that she didn't call our room."

"She only arrived today," he said, keeping his

voice low in case anyone was nearby. "Probably wants to scope out the situation first. And she's not actually expecting me until tomorrow."

Emma nodded. "So we ask Mindy for an intro, and if that doesn't pan out, we look for someone alone in the bar or restaurant."

"And if *that* yields nothing," he added, tugging her to a stop beside him, "we go back to our room and go off the clock until sun-up."

She didn't respond at first, and he almost regretted the words. He knew damn well neither one of them were ready for anything more than an island fling, and yet at the same time he could feel himself opening up, letting hope warm him to all the delicious possibilities once The Serpent was dead and this vendetta no longer ruled his life.

Not that he was ready to play house, but he couldn't deny how much he liked having Emma at his side.

The thoughts raced by in an instant, and he almost recalled the words, wanting to give her an out if he was pushing too hard or moving too fast. Apparently she didn't think he was, because she fisted her hand in the collar of his T-shirt, using it as a lever to pull him toward her. She kissed him fast and hard, then pushed him back with a grin.

"I admire a man who's always ready with an alternative plan. Especially one I agree with wholeheartedly." Her eyes danced with mischief. "After all, all work and no play…"

He stroked her cheek. "How would either of us know? As far as I can tell, we've spent our lives doing nothing but working."

"Can't argue with that."

The sun had dipped behind the foliage, leaving the path bathed in deep orange that made the palm fronds and tropical flowers glow with a vibrancy that resembled flames. He took her hand, and they continued on the path, at least until he paused at their path's intersection with two others, one leading to another cluster of cabanas and the other to the main building.

He drew her in, relieved when she responded so eagerly, opening to his touch, his kiss. It was long and slow, and he stroked his hand along her back, bare in a low-back Tee she wore without a bra. His fingers brushed her skin as their lips clashed, the kiss that had started gentle becoming almost as intense as the fire-lit sky.

After a moment, they pulled apart, both breathing hard. "We don't have to find her today," he finally said.

"True. There's no real downside to waiting until tomorrow."

"And think of the upside." He slid his fingers lower, teasing under the band of her shorts.

"You're doing a very good job convincing me." She closed her eyes, her voice heavy with desire.

"Good, because I—*wait.*"

Her eyes opened immediately, that look of lust gone, replaced by cold calculation and total professionalism. He saw her head cock, then tilt slightly to indicate the path that led toward the other cabanas. He nodded. Just the tiniest motion, but she clocked it, and he watched as she tapped out *one, two, three* on her thigh.

They turned in unison, catching a petite blonde with short-cropped hair standing in front of them holding a camera. She squeaked and jumped, falling backward against a leafy plant.

"Well, hello," Emma said, in the kind of voice she'd used with him in bed. "This might be a resort with low inhibitions, but I think taking candid shots without permission breaks all the rules." She took his hand and put it over her breast as she leaned against him, striking a pose. "But I'm sure we could work something out."

He had to hand it to her. If she hadn't spoken

first, he probably would have asked the girl what the fuck she thought she was doing. Emma had turned it around and seamlessly kept their cover.

"That's a nice offer," the woman said. "And sorry for not asking. You two looked like you'd make a good subject. So I took a few photos. To, um, get a feel for you."

"A few?" Tony said, holding out his hand. "Can I see?"

The woman licked her lips and then passed him the camera. He scanned through the images moving backward in time from the photo she'd just taken—which clearly showed his fingers dipping down the back of Emma's shorts—then a candid of him and Emma on the path, one of them walking through the foliage that surrounded the natural spring, and finally another candid of him, Emma, and Tracy Ann.

He looked up at the blonde. She appeared to be in her mid-twenties, and she was biting her lower lip. At the moment, she looked like a rabbit who wasn't sure if it should bolt or inch closer for a bit of carrot.

"So this is a hobby?" Emma asked. She'd been looking over his shoulder at the digital screen. Now she was examining the girl.

"I really didn't mean it to be a thing. Maybe I

could buy you two a drink to make up for it? I'm Thea," she added, her focus entirely on Tony as she spoke. I'm, um, the assistant at a business in the States. We deal in news. Information."

Tony met Emma's eyes. She nodded and took a step toward Thea. "I'm Kari. I came with Tony to the island. And we're both very glad to meet you."

"Why don't we head to our cabana?" Tony suggested. "We can have a drink. Talk."

Thea nodded, her curls bouncing. "That would be great. What cabana are you in?"

"It's in the Wanton section. Called the Sea View," Emma said, and to Tony's surprise, Thea looked relieved. "That's perfect."

"How did you know I was—" Tony began, then shifted the question when Thea grabbed his hand and squeezed in what he took as a warning. "—uh, going to be a good subject for your photos?"

"Well, you have the body," she said casually. "Both of you," she added, with a nod toward Emma. She slipped her other hand into Emma's. "I think we three are going to have a very good time."

CHAPTER FIFTEEN

"All right," Thea says as soon as we reach the room. "We can talk now."

"Now?" I repeat, with a sideways glance at Tony. "Why not before?"

She shrugs, looking more than a little uncomfortable. "There aren't microphones outside," she says. "But some of the staff are trained to—well, you know."

"Actually, we don't," Tony says. "Why don't you tell us?" The words are a question, but it's clear he means them as an order.

"They listen. And if they think that someone is here who might cause trouble, they report it to upper management."

"Trouble," I repeat.

Her face goes bright red. "Well, it *is* a sex resort."

My shoulders sag a bit with relief. "Reporters," I say. "People who might leak photos. Violate confidentiality."

"Right. Exactly."

"You had a camera."

She blushes. "My boss likes me to come back with souvenirs. And he's tight with the owner. So I kind of get a pass."

I grimace. "Nice to know the place abides so strictly by its own rules."

"Oh, my boss only looks at them himself. I, well, he's not big on traveling. I think it's his version of amateur porn."

"But it's safe to talk in here?" Tony presses. "No one's listening? Or looking?"

"Not here, no." Thea looks at both me and Tony in turn. "Some of the cabanas have hidden cameras and recorders," she tells us. "But this one's clean."

"Right," Tony says after coolly studying her. "Follow me."

He leads her into the small kitchen and points at the table. She sits, and I do the same. A moment later, Tony joins us with a bottle of wine. I bite back a smile. The cabana is well-stocked with alcohol, presumably for lowering sexual inhibitions. It also tends to loosen lips.

As I expect, he pours her a generous glass, then does the same for me. I hide a smile, wondering what kind of interrogation he has in store for me later tonight. Whatever it is, I imagine I'll like it.

"Okay," he says after pouring his own glass. "Tell us how you know all of this. And after that, I want to hear about The Serpent."

She takes a sip. "My boss is friends with the owner of the island. He comes here a lot, and sometimes he sends his colleagues. And competition, too. Just offers them a vacation, no strings attached."

She rolls her eyes. "But of course he makes sure the staff assigns them one of the cabanas with the microphones or cameras. He finds it useful. And since he's gotten the owner out of a few jams, he knows which cabanas are wired and which aren't."

"And you're confident in your information?"

"Do you think I'd be talking to you if I wasn't?"

Tony's face doesn't change, but his body stiffens in a way I find telling. I'm certain he's thinking what I am—this could so easily be a set up. But why? It's not as if he's ever gotten close enough to The Serpent for the assassin to suddenly decide to send Thea in order to lure us here. If The Serpent was trying to draw Tony out, there'd surely been many opportunities over the years. To The Serpent, Tony—and me, for that matter—were essentially nothing. Gnats to be ignored. The man was a ghost, after all. And it's hard to chase a ghost.

So unless he was severely breaking pattern, Thea was most likely the real deal. Someone with intel, who decided to reach out.

As for why … well, that remained to be seen.

"Who do you work for?" Tony asks.

"Harvey Dailey," she says, and I sit up a little bit straighter, recognizing the name.

While Dailey is hardly an upstanding citizen, he's not someone who's ever been in my crosshairs. As far as I know, Dailey isn't interested in buying little girls for his own personal use. Instead, he's in the business of blackmail, and he uses the various arms of his legitimate business network to launder the proceeds from those schemes.

Securities fraud and similar white collar crimes are also on the menu, but none of that ever got my juices flowing, either as a PI or when

I was in covert ops. As far as I'm concerned, paper-pushing crimes don't require my particular skill set. And if someone can be blackmailed, they're at least a little bit culpable. Not that I can't sympathize, I do. But if it's a choice between helping someone keep their illicit affair secret or rescuing a runaway who's gotten sucked into prostitution, it's really a no-brainer for me.

I glance at Tony and can tell from his expression that he recognizes the name, too. "And The Serpent?" he asks. "I suppose he works for Dailey now as well?"

That's my guess, too. That after the death of Tony's father, The Serpent signed on with a new master.

Thea nods. "Exactly."

"And now for the bonus question, Thea. What's The Serpent's real name? And how the fuck did you track me down?"

His voice is deadly calm now, every hint of lightness snuffed out. It's the first time I've really seen that side of him, and I'm impressed. Possibly more than I should be, as I realize that I'm starting to envision him as a partner, when really, I should only be thinking about him in bed. And that, only temporarily.

She takes a large gulp of her wine, swallows,

and then finishes the rest of it. Tony raises his brows, and she shrugs. "You're really kind of scary," she says, and at that moment, it hits me how young she is. Probably not even twenty-five.

"I try. Talk."

"I've worked for Dailey for a couple of years, and I've learned stuff. It's not a legitimate business. And I know that Federal agents have been sniffing around, and I've heard words like RICO and money laundering and conspiracy and stuff like that."

"Okay. Go on."

She shakes her head. "That's not me. I don't want to be part of that. But if I try to get out..." She trails off, biting her lip. "I—I told Mr. Dailey that I wanted to quit to go back to business school. And Mr. Dailey said that I should work for him while I'm getting my degree. So I told him that sounded great. Because what choice did I have?"

Tony looks at me, and I move my head in the slightest nod. The silent communication is clear. This girl is legitimately scared, and not just because her boss collects blackmail tapes and launders money. This is the fear of a bullet in the brain.

"But here you are," I say. "So what happened?"

Her throat moves as she swallows. "My brother was a hacker. Is, really, though he swears he doesn't do it much, and only to keep his skills up. But he used to be all over the dark web, digging in all sorts of creepy places. And he'd tell me about it. So once I started feeling really trapped, I thought maybe I could find out about my boss on the dark web."

"You were going to blackmail him for your job?" Tony's voice is incredulous.

She shakes her head. "Honestly, I didn't know what I was looking for. And then Billy— that's my brother—started stumbling across these questions about The Serpent. Buried queries, but all from the same guy. Turned out to be you," she says, looking at Tony.

He reaches his hand out and takes mine. "So why meet me?"

"I figured you wanted to kill him. Either that or hire him, but I doubted that. But for me, it doesn't really matter. Because I can tell you his name and where he lives, and I figure that's worth something."

"And now we get to the crux of it," Tony says. "What do you want?"

"Help," she says plaintively. "The owner of Debauchery lets my boss use his vault to keep records. Like in that Tom Cruise movie, *The Firm*. Stuff that's not on the computer because, well, people like my brother could hack in. I want to get in there, take a ton of photos, and then go to the Feds. If I have evidence of all the shit they're into, they'll protect me, right?"

"You'll end up in Witness Protection," I point out.

"Good," she says with what sounds like genuine eagerness. "I've made a mess of this life. That's what I want. A totally fresh start."

"Do they know you're here? Dailey? His people?"

She nods. "The island is a perk. Like I said, it belongs to Dailey's friend. I'm not supposed to know about the cameras, but I do. So I think when I asked to come here during my vacation, they were more than happy to let me. I'm in one of the monitored cabanas." She makes a face, and I'm assuming she's thinking about finding someone to take back with her, just to make sure her cover looks legit.

"So you're looking for our help to get into the vault? Believe it or not, we can't just crack the lock to a vault by pressing our ear to the door. This isn't an action flick."

She shakes her head. "No. I have the combination. Like I said, my boss is friends with Debauchery's owner. So he lets Dailey keep a vault here. I think they all know it's for paperwork he doesn't want the IRS to see, but nobody talks about it. And that's one of my jobs—rotating out the combination every other week. What I need is your help getting a contact in law enforcement. Someone I can trust who'll actually help me. I don't know how to reach out. I mean, Dailey has people loyal to him in the government and the court system. If I approach the wrong person, he could—"

Tony holds up a hand. "Gotcha. That's doable. And in exchange you'll tell me where to find The Serpent. And his real name?"

She nods. "I don't know either offhand. But I know it's in the vault. All the personnel records are, along with dossier's, blackmail material, that kind of thing."

Tony stands, then goes to the cutlery drawer. He takes out two steak knives, then returns and hands one to me. Not the best weapon, but if this mission is as simple as Thea is making it out to be, we won't need a weapon at all. Still, I strip off the handle to make the blade more balanced if I'm forced to use it as a weapon.

With a frown, Tony lifts Thea's wine glass. "Go take a nap. I assume you can find the bedroom? Two hours. And eat this," he adds, pulling out one of the croissants we'd found in a kitchen welcome basket."

"I'm not really—"

"I need you sharp. We do it my way or not at all. After we wake you, you can run us through it. Location of the vault. Potential surveillance. Any sort of alarm system that will need to be disengaged. Anything you can think of."

"Sure," she says, "but it won't be a big deal. I'm here for some R&R, right? And getting into the vault is just a favor for my boss."

"You're right," I say, taking my seat beside Tony. "It sounds simple. But trust me. It never, ever is. Go on," I add gently. "Get some rest. We'll wake you."

"You'll be here? With me?"

"We're going to take some coffee out on the patio. No microphones in the garden?"

"None," she says. "Save some coffee for me. I'm always groggy after a nap."

Tony laughs. "Will do." He watches her leave, then turns to me. "And how about you?"

"I don't need a nap," I say, making him laugh. Or, at least, making him grin.

"I meant it about the coffee," he adds, making us each a cup in the single-serve machine. "And the patio," he says as he passes me a cup.

I follow him outside, then sit cross-legged at the foot of the double-style lounger. "Is this where we plan the real mission?"

He shakes his head as he sits on the edge of the lounge, close enough I could reach out and touch him. I want to, but I don't. Both because we should be in work mode right now, and because I'm frustrated by my own desire. This low, buzzing need to reach out to him. To feel that connection that has been strangely, uncomfortably, amazingly growing since he waltzed into my house and convinced me that he truly wanted me on this job.

"What's going on," I press as he stays silent. "Are you worried about Thea? She seems—"

"I'm going to sign on at Stark Security."

"Oh." I want to say more, but every word I ever knew is stuck in my throat. "That's great. You'll be an amazing asset."

"It occurred to me that they'll probably match us up as partners. Especially after this mission."

I lift a shoulder. "I suppose. Is that a problem?" I can't keep the edge out of my voice. Or the anger out of the words that tumble out. "Because if you're worried that I'll get all possessive and strange just because we tumbled around naked, don't worry. We had a good time, you're a great fuck, and I'm sure you'll be an awesome partner, too."

A muscle in his cheek twitches, but his eyes are flat. At first he says nothing. Then he nods. "Right. Well, cool. I guess we're good then. I hope we do work together. You've got serious skills."

"Back at you," I say, fuming a bit and hating myself for it. Why is it so easy to burst into a room I know is full of armed morons and yet I can't manage to tell this guy that even though I don't understand why, he means more to me than a casual fuck?

He hesitates, and I think maybe he's going to say something. But then he stands and turns and heads for the door.

Good. Great. Terrific. Relationships are messy and complicated and confusing. Not something I've ever aspired to, and not something I need now.

Which is a big fat lie, and since my biggest

rule is to never lie to Eliza or myself, I am all sorts
of confused at the moment.

And that emotional status devolves into a
whirlwind of hope and teenage-girlish angst
when he stops at the doorway, turns around, and
says harshly, "Fuck it."

"Excuse me?" I snap back, but he ignores my
tone, and thank God for that. He crosses over the
flagstones in two long strides, grabs my upper
arms, and hauls me to my feet.

"Hey!"

"Just let me get this out and then you can
ream me nine ways from Sunday. But I'm falling
for you, dammit. And I am this close—*this close*—
to nailing that son-of-a-bitch Serpent. Which
means I'm about to have a life again, maybe for
the first time. And maybe I'm an idiot, but I want
you in it. As my partner," he says. "On the job
and off."

"Good God. Is this a proposal?"

He actually bursts out laughing. "If you
could see your face."

I reach for his hand. "Wait," I say, though
he's not going anywhere. Maybe my face did look
confused, but I guess I didn't look terrified or
horrified, because he seems to know I don't want

him to go. Hell, he seems to have figured it out even before I did.

"Wait?" he repeats, softer now. "What am I waiting for?"

"For my apology?" I draw a breath, then let it out slowly. "Everything you just said. Ditto."

His mouth curves into a vibrant smile. "And I thought men were supposed to be the taciturn ones."

"Yeah, well, how's this. I'm sorry I played turtle and dove into myself. If you do something scary like pull out a ring, I'll dive right back in again. But this—what you're suggesting, I mean. Being partners in work and in life. Being together. Yeah. I don't know why, but I want to try it."

"Thanks a lot."

I grin. "Fair enough. I do know why. It's you. You snuck into my heart when I wasn't expecting it. Wouldn't be fair to kick you out without giving you a fair shot."

He rolls his eyes and tugs me to my feet. "Emma?"

"Yes?"

"Stop talking." And then, thank goodness, he kisses me.

CHAPTER SIXTEEN

As far as Tony was concerned, this was one of the craziest missions he'd ever been on. But it was all worth it to have Emma in his arms, that sassy mouth on his, and her body pressed close.

With a low moan, he deepened the kiss, pulling her down until they were prone on the lounge chair. She made a soft noise of protest, then broke the kiss, propping herself up on an elbow to look at him.

One lock of hair escaped from where she'd tucked it behind her ear, and the strands brushed his cheek as she said, "We can't now. We need to get going."

"Oh, I think we can." He grinned, then

flipped them over, making her squeal as she landed flat on the cushion with him straddling her. Now her hair was splayed out, and in the twinkling lights that decorated the patio, she looked like an angel. *His* angel, he thought, and instead of corny, that silly and sentimental thought seemed sweet. And true.

"Tony..."

Her voice held an admonishment, but her hands—which were skimming lightly down his back to cup his ass—told a different story.

"She's asleep. No harm in letting her get in a few more minutes."

"Sounds like a justification to me."

"I'll justify most anything to be with you."

She laughed. "Nice line, but not true. You wouldn't sacrifice our chance to get in that vault, and you wouldn't sacrifice her safety."

All true. God, she already knew him so well. "I wouldn't sacrifice you, either," he added.

"Not an issue. I can take care of myself."

"You definitely can." He shifted his weight so that he could use one hand to trail lightly over her body, then focused on teasing her breast through the thin material of her shirt. "Right now, though, I want to take care of you."

"I like that plan," she whispered, and he

could tell she meant it from the way her pulse had kicked up and the small sounds of pleasure she made as he lightly stroked her.

He moved forward, gently brushing his lips over hers, then easing down to taste the curve of her jaw before moving lower still.

"Wait." The word was soft, barely a whisper, but it sent a cold rush of fear running through him. Not because she wanted to stop, but because he wanted to continue so badly. Wanted *her* so badly. And though she'd just told him that she wanted him, too, he still couldn't quite believe it.

He said nothing, but he felt more vulnerable than he could ever remember. Even back when he was a kid at his father's mercy. Or later on a mission, trapped in a corner with some asshole's gun aimed at his head.

He'd survived then. He wasn't sure if he'd survive now if she backed off of her earlier words and told him this was just an island fling. That there wasn't anything real between them. Nothing worth exploring, even if just to see if they'd stick.

"I'm not..." she began, and he felt a cold, hard hand tighten around his heart.

She cleared her throat and started over. "I'm

not sure how to do this. How to make this work. You and me, I mean."

Her eyes were wide and earnest, and she looked soft and innocent and completely trusting. And that's when he knew that they had a shot. Because there was no trace of the badass woman who could break his neck if she wanted to. She was showing him her weak side, and for a woman like Emma, that said a hell of a lot more than words.

He held her gaze and heard the hint of suppressed joy in his voice as he said simply, "Nothing to it. It's just me being me, and you being you. And us taking it one day at a time together."

"I like that." She drew in a breath, her brow furrowing. "Listen, I was seeing someone before."

He shoved down the flash of jealousy. "Do I need to worry about getting my ass kicked when we get back?"

Her hands on his ass gave him a little squeeze. "No. No, we broke up about three months ago. It was only casual, anyway. More like friends with benefits." She frowned again. "Well, I thought it was. She wanted more."

He nodded, but said nothing. He could see

that she had more to say, and he hoped she wasn't afraid that he'd be freaked by the fact that she'd dated a woman. He didn't care who she was with before, so long as when they were together she was with him alone.

"I just..." She trailed off, then drew in breath. "I can't believe I'm saying this out loud. Shit." Another deep breath then she blurted, "It's only that this time—with you—I'm a little bit afraid that I'll be the one who wants more."

Glorious relief swelled in his chest. "Sweetheart, you don't have anything to worry about there."

"You've gotten under my skin," she said. "You're in my head."

He kissed her lightly, then grinned. "Sounds uncomfortable."

"Honestly, it's surprisingly cozy." She swallowed. "I don't feel like this often. No, that's a lie," she corrected, and he bit back a wince, afraid she was about to tell him of a long, lost love she pined for.

Since he was distracted, it was easy for her to get the better of him, which she did by moving fast and flipping him over, causing him to both gasp and laugh as she straddled him. "The truth is, I've never felt like this. So don't break my heart, ok?"

She slid her hands up so she was cupping his throat, her thumbs positioned so that it wouldn't take much effort to crush his windpipe. "I was trained by a secret government agency, remember?" Her voice was low and teasing, but there was truth there, too. "Trust me when I say that I can think of a lot of on-theme ways to get revenge for a broken heart."

"I'll keep that in mind." He bent up, ignoring the brief pressure on his throat before she moved her hands. Then he kissed her, his fingers moving to slide off her shorts.

"Ah-ah," she chided. "If we get in that vault, get the info, and get back here in under two hours, I will fuck you so hard you'll see stars. But right now, we have a mission."

"Yes, we do. And," he added setting the timer on his watch, "the clock is ticking."

"Mario didn't get any hits," Emma told Tony about an hour later. They'd pulled a set of prints and sent them to the SSA tech guru. "He admits it's hardly a full check, but without a last name, there's not more he can do in such a short time. We know Dailey must be dirty, or else why the private vault?As for Thea..."

She trailed off with a shrug, and he nodded agreement. "She either is or she isn't, but under the circumstances, we're going to go with it. Stay sharp."

"Always," she'd said, then kissed him, her lips lingering on his even once Thea had entered the room. Then she'd pulled away and winked. "Just claiming what's mine," she'd said before taking his hand and nodding toward Thea. "Let's roll."

Now they were moving down one of the paths that led to the island's boathouse, which was kept locked after sunset. The paths remained open for guests to stroll, however, and as the three of them did their best to look casual, they kept an eye out for anyone else who might be wandering nearby. So far, he'd seen no one.

"The vault is attached to the backside of the boathouse," Thea told them. "It looks like an old maintenance area, but it's a serious stronghold."

Tony saw what she meant once they were off the main walkway and moving down a narrower path that circled around to the back. The exterior was battered and rusty corrugated metal. The concrete of the ramp into the water was cracked and buckling. As Thea had said, the area appeared to have been cast aside in favor of the shiny new maintenance dock they'd seen as they'd approached the boat house.

He met Emma's eyes, saw her quick nod as if to say, *Clever. Very clever.*

Thea opened the battered, rusty door to reveal a formidable steel plate. "It slides open," she said, then moved past Tony as she reached for the breaker box.

It wasn't really a breaker box, of course. Instead, it had a false front that, when opened, revealed an electronic keypad. She closed her eyes, sang a few numbers under her breath, then faced him and Emma with a shrug. "I was scared to write them down. Songs trigger memory, did you know?"

"Smart," Emma said. "Assuming you remembered the lyrics right."

Thea grinned. "We'll see," she said, then tapped in the code.

Almost immediately, they heard a hydraulic hiss, then the slow slide of the door to the left. Tony nodded, impressed, and ushered Thea inside.

"Pull the metal door shut," Thea said as Emma started in behind them. "There's a panel in here, too, but it creeps me out to have the vault door closed. But we'll want to turn on the lights."

"I'll get it," Emma said, then tugged the corrugated door shut as Thea flipped the switch to turn on the single, dim bulb that swung in a cage above them.

Even in the minimal lighting, Tony could make out the room. A desk. A pad of paper. A printer. No computer, though. He assumed anyone working in the vault was expected to bring their own laptop.

Around them, every wall was lined with metal filing cabinets, their edges starting to rust despite the sealed nature of the vault.

"Over here," Thea said, then hurried to the middle cabinet on the far side of the room. "This is where all the independent contractors—"

She cut herself off as she pulled open a file drawer. Then she yanked open the one above and the one below, her movements becoming more and more frantic until, finally, she turned to look at Tony and Emma. "It's empty," she said. "There's nothing in these drawers at all."

"*Shit.*" Tony spit out the curse, even as he pulled open the file drawers closest to him.

Behind him, he could hear Emma doing the same.

"They moved everything," Thea said as she turned to look at him. "Why would they do that without telling me?"

Tony pulled the steak knife from his pocket, noticing Emma was doing the same. "Either they didn't tell you because it didn't matter. You weren't coming here for work, after all. Just a vacation."

"But—"

"Or," Emma continued, stepping over Thea's protest, "they don't trust you. And this is a trap."

"No, no. They trust me. I know they do. I—" She cut herself off with a groan, then ran her fingers through her hair. "I don't understand."

"Right now, we don't have to," Tony said. "All we need to do is get out of here."

He gestured for Emma to take the lead as he gripped Thea's upper arm. He wasn't certain what had gone sideways, but he intended to keep her close.

Emma exited first, then Tony and Thea. She hurried to the control panel, punched in the code, and the door slid shut. Tony moved the corrugated door back in place, and the three of them stepped out from under the overhang—and the moment they did, a tall, thin figure moved onto the path a few yards in front of them.

He wore a baseball cap that kept the moonlight from hitting his face, keeping his features hidden in the shadows. But he was smiling, white teeth gleaming. Immediately, Emma was at Tony's side, both of them standing as a barrier between Thea and this stranger.

"Don't bother with that," the man said, his voice a low rumble. "I'm not here to hurt Thea. I'm here to thank her. She led me to you, after all. It's so nice to meet you, Antonio, after so many yearsssssss." He drew out the *s*, as if Tony hadn't already figured out his identity. As if Tony's blood hadn't already started to boil from the heat of his fury.

The Serpent. Standing right the fuck in front of him after all these years.

"You killed my mother," Tony said.

"She begged for her life. Not your uncle. He at least died with dignity, but not before telling me I'd suffer." He indicated himself. "So far, no suffering."

Behind him, Thea was murmuring, "No, no," and he realized the same words were running through his head. *No no no no no.*

Emma reached for his hand and squeezed it,

and he resisted the urge to close his eyes. But he let himself soak in her strength. Her power. And when he lifted his chin and looked The Serpent in the face again, he felt a bit calmer. There was only one of the bastard, and together Tony and Emma were formidable.

It just might be possible...

In front of him, The Serpent extended his hand. "Thea, my girl. You did everything perfectly. Come here."

"She's not going anywhere," Tony said, angling his body so that he could grab Thea's arm and hold tight. "Not until I have answers."

"Fine," The Serpent said, then drew a pistol and aimed it at Emma. "Either you send Thea trotting over here, or Red gets two in the chest."

"He will," Thea said. "Please, please, don't give him a reason to hurt Kari."

Barely a foot away, Emma stood unmoving. There was no cover, nowhere to go. And they both knew The Serpent was a stellar shot.

She turned her head just enough so Tony could see her face. She didn't have a plan—that much was obvious.

What was also obvious was that she trusted him to handle this.

But Christ, the thought of putting a civilian into The Serpent's hands...

"It's okay," Thea said, apparently understanding his dilemma. "He won't hurt me."

She started to take a step toward The Serpent, but Tony grabbed her arm and held her back. "No," he said. "Just stay right here."

The Serpent laughed. "Idiot. She's right to trust me. After all, I'm the one who sent her here."

"The hell you did," Tony countered, even as Thea said, "Only to get the records for you."

It took him a moment to realize that when Thea said *for you*, she meant *for The Serpent*. Not *for Tony*.

"Thea?" Emma voiced the question first, but it was to Tony that Thea addressed the answer. "I —I was supposed to give him your records so you could find him after all these years. He wanted the two of you to finally have it out."

A tear trickled down her cheek. "He said he wanted it over."

She sniffled, then faced The Serpent. "You weren't supposed to be here," she snapped. "You said if I came and got the information and gave it to him, that was it. That I could leave and we'd call it even."

He chuckled, the sound both harsh and amused. "Darling, Thea. You really shouldn't put so much stock in pillow talk. I'll say almost anything for a quality fuck."

"You prick!" She burst away from Tony and even as he reached out to yank her back, the Serpent shifted his stance and as he fired,

Tony was reminded the silencers in real life are nothing like the movies.

Dozens of birds shot upwards from their shelter in the trees to flap and caw in the dark sky as Thea stumbled and fell to the ground, the two quick shots hitting her dead in the chest and shoulder.

Tony raced to her side, wincing when he saw the wounds. It was bad—very bad, and he pressed his hands over them, trying to staunch the flow of blood.

"Idiot bitch," The Serpent said. "Just like that one," he added, training the gun on Emma, who'd moved to stand by Tony. "Another one who's good with the pillow talk, just like me."

"You fucker," Tony snarled. "She's nothing like you."

"No? Then maybe you can tell me why she works for Dailey, too."

"What the hell?" Emma's voice was practically a snarl. "What kind of a fucked up game are you—"

"Dailey hired her to take out Billy Cane. Cane's been skimming funds, and our Emma's been working for Dailey for years cleaning up those kinds of messes."

"Tony," she said. "No."

But he couldn't hear her, not really. Not with The Serpent yammering and Thea gasping as he pressed hard, keeping pressure on the wound.

"But I can solve that problem," The Serpent said, twisting toward Emma. "I can do that little thing for you and get rid of the bitch." As he spoke, he lifted the gun, ignoring Tony's shout for him to stop, to stop, to just fucking stop.

A split second later, The Serpent was howling, the gun clattering to the ground as blood flowed from the gash on his wrist. It took a second for Tony to process what had happened, but then he realized that Emma had hurled the steak knife into his flesh—the remarkable accuracy a testament to her skills—and then vaulted across the space so that she was now almost at The Serpent's side. She thrust up with her leg, catching him under the chin and forcing him to stumble back as she dove for the gun.

He managed to recover and kicked it away,

sending it tumbling into the underbrush. Emma dove for it—and The Serpent spun and bolted down the path, long legs churning. Seconds later, the roar of a small boat engine fired, the sound disappearing as the craft sped away.

Emma stood there, gun in hand, her chest heaving as she shook her head. "It's not true. None of it. Dammit, Tony. Tell me you know it's not true."

He didn't want to believe it. He couldn't believe it. So he ignored it—for now. "Call the main building. Tell them to get a medical team here."

"No service," she said, looking at her phone. "I'll go." Then she was gone, sprinting through the trees to the main house. And somehow Tony knew that she wouldn't come back. He'd fucked up. For a moment—just a moment—he'd let himself believe the worst. And not even about her, not really.

No, what he'd feared was that he'd lost his edge. That he'd spent so many years looking only for The Serpent hidden in the shadows, that he'd been unable to see real danger when it stood in front of him in the light.

But Emma ... oh, God, Emma. How could he

have entertained such a horrible thought even for a second?

"It's true." The small, weak voice came from Thea. He'd taken off his shirt to try to staunch the blood, and now the cloth and his hands were soaked as he kept pressure on the wound, and he smiled down at her, murmuring bullshit about how she shouldn't talk. That it would be okay.

"It's true," she repeated. "He...told me. Before. You're...her...mark." She gasped for air, blood bubbling at her lips.

"Just hush. Save your strength."

"I was s-supposed to tell you. Wh-when we were alone."

"Why?" He couldn't help asking the question, and immediately shifted. "No, no, stay quiet. Save your strength."

"Your...father," she whispered, as he heard the distant sound of a Jeep engine.

He called out for them, urging them to hurry, then focused again on the girl. "What about my father?"

"A—live...father...Morgan. He's...alive." For a moment, her eyes went wide. "Forgive...me?"

He sat stunned, never releasing the pressure even though he wanted to scream, to cry, to pound hard against something. But he nodded, even as tears streamed down his face. "Yeah," he said as he felt the last breath of life leave her.

As the paramedics sprinted around the corner to tend to the dead, Tony took a step back, realizing now that he had a new mission—to find his father.

And that, once again, he was all alone.

CHAPTER SEVENTEEN

"**B**ut that's ridiculous," Eliza says, as I pace in front of her. If she and Quincy had carpeting, I would have worn a path in it by now. As it is, I'm doing a good job of polishing their hardwood floor with my bare feet. "There's no way that Tony could believe you were working with either The Serpent or this Dailey guy."

"Really? Because he seemed pretty damn ready to believe." And why wouldn't he? The Serpent knew about the Cane mission. And how the hell would he know that if I wasn't somehow working with him or his handler. "*Fuck,*" I say, then repeat it three more times just because it feels good.

"But if you—"

"Dammit," I say, as I once again reach the

wall unit full of books, a stereo system, and old LPs. "This place is too damn small." This is why I have the bungalow. I have a condo, too—it was the first place I bought when I had a bit of money, but I turned it into a rental right away. The bungalow has room to move. Small spaces leave me feeling trapped and antsy. Maybe they remind me of our utility room, I don't know. But I had to move back into the condo a few months ago while I was having some work done on the bungalow, and I couldn't believe Eliza and I had lived there for over a year back in the day. It seemed so cramped. And being boxed in just doesn't work for me.

Maybe that's it. Maybe that's why this goddamn accusation pisses me off so much. Because The Serpent boxed me in, and I can't even find him and throttle him and make him tell Tony the truth because the son-of-a-bitch is finally, truly dead—and I didn't even get the satisfaction of watching him bleed out.

I got confirmation this morning that a small motorboat had drifted onto the beach of a nearby island. In it was a dead man dressed in black and wearing a baseball cap. He'd died from bullet wounds—two in the chest and one in the head. I'd retrieved the gun and caught up with him as he was pulling away from the doc. I'd got off three shots. Apparently, they'd found their way home.

"At least you killed him," Eliza says, reading my mind as always. "That's something."

I make a scoffing noise. "Yeah, Tony will assume I did it because The Serpent rattled off the truth and pissed me off. *And* he'll be annoyed because he's been gunning to kill the bastard for years, and now I've denied him the pleasure."

"Yeah, but otherwise the guy would have escaped. I mean, Tony's not an idiot, right? He has to know—"

"He thinks I lied to him. That I'm lying to the SSA. Dammit, Eliza, he thinks I'm one of the bad guys."

My sister's brows rise to her hairline and she sinks back into the cushions. "Sorry. Shit. Don't bite my head off."

Fuck. Fuck, fuck, fuckety-fuck.

With a sigh, I drop into a cushy, leather armchair. One of the few pieces of furniture that makes me remember that Quince is British, since it seems like something you'd find in the scene-of-the-crime library featured in an Agatha Christie novel.

When I look up, I find my sister staring at me. I sigh. "What?"

"This isn't like you. There's something else going on."

"More than my partner thinking I'm a turn-coat who's aligned with a criminal prick that the SOC and half a dozen other intelligence agencies wanted to capture alive? No, I think that's plenty to be going on."

"Dammit, Emma, it's me."

I bite back yet another curse, then sigh loudly. "I just don't..." I trail off, letting my hand rise and fall on the armrest in silent testament to the futility of this entire conversation.

"I liked him, okay?" The words are clipped. Harsh enough that they sound like a challenge. Anyone else would have cowered. My sister does the opposite, leaning forward eagerly, her eyes wide.

"Define *like*," she demands.

"I'm not a sixth-grader, and we are not playing that game."

"Did you sleep with him?"

I cock my head. "Hello? Sex island. What do you think?"

"Fair enough. But you also know what I

mean. You're not exactly celibate, and you don't fall in love with everyone you sleep with."

I pull my legs up so that I'm sitting cross-legged in the armchair. "That's because I don't think sex is some transcendental experience. Recreation is a perfectly acceptable reason for getting naked."

"Not disagreeing. Except sometimes it's more than that." She props her chin on her fist, studying me as I stay silent. "It was more than that, wasn't it?"

"I don't know him well enough for it to be more than that."

She just smiles.

And again I think, *fuck*.

I draw a breath. "Fine. *Fine*. Truth? I don't know how I feel about him. Okay, no. That's not true. I'm pissed as hell. I connected with him, El." I hear myself and want to wince, because I sound weak and lost and confused, and that is not who I am. And that makes me even more pissed because Antonio Fucking Santos is the one who made me this way.

"Talk to him," she says. "Maybe you're wrong. I can't believe he would think that of you. I mean, *you*. You'd never align yourself with people like that."

"He must have believed it. Why else didn't he come looking for me? I was on the island all night. I got on the first shuttle off the next morning, but I was there in one of the cabanas until morning. He could have had the front desk leave me a message. Hell, he could have met me at the runway. But he didn't come, he didn't call. He believed The Serpent. He believed that low-life, murderous scum over me."

She says nothing. Just sits back with a frown. For a solid minute the silence hangs between us, and it feels like a year. "You told him. You told him about us. Our life. And about you getting arrested. About getting recruited. Emma, you told this guy all of that?"

I don't answer, but I know she can see my throat move as I swallow, and her shoulders sag under the weight of my silent confession.

"I'm sorry," she says, and for the first time, I'm certain that she really and truly gets it. Because I never open up that much to anyone. And the fact that I did—and then he looked at me with such cold horror...

This really shouldn't hurt so much. I'm tougher than this. Or, at least, I thought I was.

With a sigh, I untangle my legs and stand up. "I don't know. Maybe I deserve it. The truth is, I didn't tell him everything. I never told him the SOC's been after The Serpent. Or that I wanted him dead as well. For all he knows, I'd never heard of the asshole before."

"Not exactly relevant to him hurting your heart."

"Isn't it? Karma's a bitch, right?" I frown, thinking about all the reasons Karma has to punish me. After all, that wasn't the only thing I held back from Tony. I never told him about his father, either. About how Clyde Morgan was the one who'd arranged to buy me and Eliza on the black market. But since that's the one secret I've kept from Eliza, too, I don't mention it now.

"You're frowning."

"Gee. I wonder why."

She tilts her head, and I scramble to cover. "I was thinking of Thea. The poor girl is dead."

"You said she was in bed with The Serpent. Literally and figuratively."

I nod. "True enough. But I don't think she had a choice. She got sucked into the quicksand and was trying to find a way out." I meet my sister's eyes. "That could have been either one of our stories."

Eliza nods. "Yeah. And you're the reason it's not. You took care of both of us."

I manage a smile and a soft, "I guess." But what she says is only the partial truth. It wasn't just me. It was Seagrave and the SOC. Because I did get sucked into the quicksand and the system was ready to take me out of the game entirely. They gave me back my life and set me up with a solid career.

And now, because of me, one of the criminals they most wanted to bring in and interrogate is dead.

I'm definitely not batting a thousand.

Eliza stands and pulls me into a hug. "I'm sorry about Tony. Do you want to stay for dinner? Quince'll be home in a couple of hours. We could have spaghetti and watch some ridiculous action movie with spies, and you two can spend the entire show complaining about how it's not realistic at all."

"Wow. It's like you know us so well. But no. I need to get home."

"Call if you need me. Any time."

"I know," I say, then hug her tight again. "Listen, El," I begin as we break apart.

"Yeah?"

I wave the words away. "Nothing." I want to ask how long it took before she knew that Quince was the guy for her, but I already know the answer. She knew within minutes of meeting him in a London park.

It had been true insta-love. Until he fucked up, anyway. But at least he fixed it.

I'm not sure if what I'm feeling is love or lust or something else entirely. But I know it hurts.

And I haven't got a clue how to fix it.

CHAPTER EIGHTEEN

I'd biked from my bungalow to Quince and Eliza's Santa Monica condo, and by the time I've cycled back home, the physical exertion and sunshine have cleared my head a bit, if not completely lifted my mood.

The bottom line is that I withheld stuff from Tony. The SOC's interest in The Serpent. My interest in Tony's father.

I didn't tell him any of that because I've never trusted anyone except Eliza.

I guess Tony doesn't really trust either. God knows he didn't trust me. And our mutual lack of trust is hardly the basis of a relationship. Hell, I'm not sure it's a basis for anything.

The thought depresses me more than it should. Especially since it's better this way. Even though *this way* means that he's undoubtedly out of my life forever.

Thoughts of Tony and the island—the good, the *very* good, and the bad—spin in my mind in time with the cadence of my pedals, and it's a relief when I finally get home. I store my bike in my tiny garage, then head straight for the shower. I'm just toweling off when the doorbell rings. I reach automatically for my phone to check the camera feed, then remember I tossed it on the kitchen table when I entered.

I tell myself it couldn't possibly be Tony, though I really hope it is. Since I don't want to admit to that hope—not even to myself—I pull on a pair of grungy sweatpants and an ancient Dave Matthews Band concert Tee. The print is almost unreadable and the collar is ripped. If this outfit doesn't convey that I'm completely blasé about who is at my door, nothing will.

I call out that I'm coming as I hurry in that direction, still in bare feet. Most important of all, I'm refusing to acknowledge the tingle of antici-pation. It's not like me, and as far as I'm concerned, it's an inconvenient and unremark-able anomaly.

I reach the door, check the small, eye-level

monitor, and feel my entire body sag with disappointment.

I take a second to regroup, then plaster on a smile as I open the door to Winston, who's standing casually on my door step in jeans and a button-down he's tucked in over a white T-shirt.

"Get in here," I hiss, then follow that up with, "Are you insane," once he's inside and the door is closed behind him. "What if someone saw you?"

"Let them look. You're SSA now, remember? And I'm here on official business."

I relax, then drag my fingers through my hair as I head back to the kitchen. "Right. Sorry. Today's been a bitch, and yesterday was worse. Whiskey?" I ask as he takes a seat at one of the stools that surround the kitchen island.

"Got any beer?"

"I have the real deal," I tell him, then pull out a Guinness. "Not that watered down piss that you drink."

"Whiskey," he amends. "Neat."

I pour one for each of us, then lean against the counter by the sink. "So what's going on? Did Ryan pair us for a mission?" I could handle that. Winston's low key and perpetually cool—until he's not. He's the kind of guy no one sees coming. Like Liam Neeson in *Taken*. All slow and easy at the beginning—maybe even a little nerdy and unsure—and then a total bad ass when it counts.

"Yeah, that was a bit of bullshit. I'm not here about anything to do with the SSA. But," he adds, holding up a finger before I can ream him a new one, "you *are* new, and it makes sense I'd come welcome you. We can pretend I brought this whiskey." He takes another sip. "I've got damn good taste."

"Come on, man. Whatever this is, can we do it later. I had a shit day. I want to go to bed and wake up in another decade."

"Seagrave told me what happened."

I cross my arms over my chest and frown. "And you're here why? I've already been debriefed. Time to move on." I'd gone straight from the airport to the SOC and told my former boss everything. Well, everything relevant. Seagrave wasn't thrilled that The Serpent was dead, but under the circumstances, he had to concede that I'd done the right thing.

"Give it up, Emma. You don't have to constantly play the bad ass. I've known you too long."

"I *am* a bad ass. It's not a role. And I just mean that it's over. It's done. Moving on might require an official debrief but it doesn't need two hours on a couch for psychoanalysis. Not with the department shrink and not even with a well-meaning friend."

"At least you acknowledge I'm well-meaning." He finishes off his whiskey, then pulls a pack of gum out and pops a stick in his mouth. He told me once that he'd never smoked until he had to start for an undercover job. He ended up addicted to the stuff. Now, when he feels the urge, he chews spearmint gum.

I guess my less than sunshiny personality is triggering a craving. Probably not my finest hour.

"I'm just making sure you're okay. And since we're now both gainfully employed by the same entity, I can do that. We can let our love run free. Cue the violins. No more hiding in the closet."

I have to fight a smile as I say, "Don't be funny. It doesn't suit you."

"Seriously, he told me about the mission. The girl. Tony."

I stiffen. "What did he tell you about Tony?"

"Just that The Serpent made you out to look dirty." He shakes his head. "You shouldn't have bolted. From what Quince and Liam say, Antonio Santos isn't the kind of guy that would believe that. Not after he spent time working with you."

"You didn't see his face."

He hesitates, then nods. "Fair enough. In that case, you doing okay with that?"

I shrug. "Nothing to be okay with. We got the job done. It was a one-time thing. I was on loan-out by order of Damien Stark. Or hadn't you heard?" It's only when I hear the harshness in my voice that I realize just how irritated I am. Damien Stark got me into this. He's the reason I was on that damn island, and if he'd never tossed my name in the hat, my heart wouldn't be bruised.

"In other words," Winston says, "you're not okay."

"Dammit, the mission went south. Am I supposed to be doing a celebratory jig?" I finish off my whiskey and pour another. I start to refill his glass, but he puts his hand over it. "Not a good mix with the spearmint."

"Remind me to never start smoking," I say dryly, making him laugh.

"I get why you're frustrated," he says, clearly not talking about cigarettes. "But the outcome was solid. The Serpent's dead, just like you wanted. And there won't be any official blowback."

"Are you finished?"

"Yeah," he says.

I come around the island to stand beside him. "Thanks. I'm glad we went through hell together back then." I manage a crooked smile. "It's nice to know I've got someone here watching out for me."

"You've always been there for me."

His words are simple, but I can hear the sadness. I almost tell him how sorry I am about everything that went down all those years ago. But I stay silent. He already knows all of that.

"Mostly I'm glad you signed on the dotted line," he continues. "The SSA's a good organization. It's starting to feel like home to me."

"I'm glad," I tell him. "Do you want to stay for a while? Hang out and watch a movie or something?"

"Nah. I'm supposed to swing by Leah's."

"Mission?"

He shakes his head. "Broken dishwasher. But she promised she'd order pizza for dinner, so I figured it was a fair trade."

I walk with him to the door, and when he pulls it open, there's Tony's Land Rover parked right across the street. With Tony himself sitting behind the wheel.

I force myself to ignore him despite the way

my body's tightening and tiny moths are starting to awaken in my belly. I stretch up to kiss Winston on his scruffy cheek. "Thanks for coming by. Seriously. It means a lot."

"Want me to bend you over and kiss you properly?"

I grimace. "I forget that the reason you were Sheriff of that podunk county wasn't just because of that sexy Texas drawl. You've got brains, too."

"So no movie finale kiss? Damn."

"Funny man."

He chuckles, apparently agreeing with my assessment. "Listen, do me a favor. I get that you're pissed at him, but don't kill him. You can't imagine the paperwork when you kill a fellow SSA agent."

"He hasn't signed on, remember?"

Winston's grin reaches all the way to his eyes. "In that case, do your worst."

I shake my head, amused, as he walks to his Ford Pickup. I wave as he drives off, then shift my attention to Tony, silently daring him to say something, get out of the car, anything.

Nothing.

So I go back inside, close my door, and head back to the kitchen to find my phone.

CHAPTER NINETEEN

Tony didn't know what the hell he was doing.

Or, rather, he did know. He was acting like a confused teenager, too scared to go talk to the pretty girl because she might slam the door in his face.

Odds were good that's exactly what would happen. Hell, she'd done that much in spirit if not in action when she'd kissed Winston good-bye, stared right at Tony, and then gone back inside without so much as a wave.

And here he was, still sitting behind the wheel, debating whether he should stay or go, like he'd been transported into a damn song by The Clash.

Fuck. Tomorrow would have been better. He

knew her flight had gotten in late last night. He should give her a day to chill.

He'd taken the late flight, arriving in LA just a few hours ago. He'd come straight here from the airport. Honestly, he'd probably fare a lot better if he showered before trying to talk to her.

Not that he'd decided what to say. Maybe he'd fucked up. But it had been a fucked up situation, and she'd bolted. Hard-as-nails Emma Tucker with her killer marksmanship and license to kill had turned and run and hadn't looked back.

His fingers ached, and he realized he was clenching the steering wheel so hard he'd probably leave an impression. Apparently, he was still pissed, repeatedly telling himself he needed to be calm when he talked to her.

So, yeah. Better to go home, shower, and try again tomorrow.

He was about to put the vehicle in drive when, somebody rapped on his window.

He turned his head and found himself staring at a skinny torso in a yellow jersey. The kid bent down, revealing sun-streaked blond hair and just a smattering of acne.

He rolled down the window, and the teen

gave him an awkward smile. "Um, you're Tony, right?"

"That depends on who's asking."

"I—um—Greg," the kid said, pointing to the name stitched on the Jersey. "I don't get many deliveries to cars. Here you go." And he held up a white bag with the logo of a popular local hamburger joint printed on the side. "So, enjoy your burger and fries. Oh, and—" He bent over and pulled a large cup up from below Tony's line of sight. Presumably an ice chest. "Almost forgot the shake."

"Do I pay?" Tony tried to keep the amusement out of his voice.

"Nah. Done online. The tip, too. Nice. So thanks."

"Wasn't me. But you're welcome."

The kid shrugged. "Guess someone's looking out for you."

"Yeah," Tony said. "You could say that."

He leaned back in the seat, leaving the window down as he opened the bag and pulled out a fry. It was like a bite of crispy heaven, and he followed it up with a swallow of frozen nirvana. "So today it is," he said to his reflection in the rearview mirror.

He grabbed the shake and the bag, rolled up

the window, then killed the engine. He got out of
the Land Rover and walked across the street,
clicking the remote to lock the car as he went.

When he reached Emma's door, he rang the
bell. He'd done this before, under slightly similar
circumstances. Only then she'd been more
annoyed at Damien than at him.

He was prepared for her to ignore the bell.
Or to speak through the intercom and tell him to
get lost.

He wasn't prepared for the shock to his
system when she opened the door. She'd pulled
her hair up into a messy ponytail. Her T-shirt
had a ripped collar and had been washed so
many times the band logo looked like little more
than a shadow. As for the sweatpants, they
looked to be at least two sizes too large, and were
tied low on her hips. She looked like someone
settling in for a day of heavy cleaning.

Mostly, though, she looked absolutely
stunning.

He started to speak, realized his mouth and
throat were completely dry, and had to start all
over again. As he struggled, she just stood there,
her arms crossed over her chest, saying nothing.

"Can we talk?"

"No." She took a step back and started to

close the door. He toed his way into the space, determined not to cringe under her wrath of God stare.

"Thanks for the burger. I would have liked cheese, but the fries and the shake made up for that oversight."

"It wasn't an oversight." Her arms stayed crossed, but she tilted her head. She did that a lot when she was amused.

"No?"

"I didn't think you deserved cheese."

"Would have to be a pretty serious crime to deprive someone of cheese. Maybe something that rises to the level of, oh, skipping out on a guy without a backward glance and leaving orders with the resort staff that she doesn't want to see him or be on the same plane off the island with him. Considering the paramedics found me with a dead resort guest, your instructions didn't exactly foster a calm and soothing manner in the way the resort staff treated me."

"And yet here you are."

He shrugged. That was true enough. "You bolted," he said flatly. "You didn't say a word to me. You just bolted."

"And say what? Gee, it was fun fucking you.

Too bad you really believed that I was working with that slimy sack of shit."

"I didn't—"

"Don't you *dare* deny it," she snapped. "I saw your face. That slithering prick implied that I'd slept with him—flat out stated I worked for his boss—and you weren't sure. For a moment there, you actually believed him."

"*Bullshit.*"

She stared him down. He congratulated himself on not cowering. She had one hell of an intimidating stare. "Go on."

"I didn't react because I believed him. Maybe I considered it only to dismiss it, and maybe that showed on my face. But you don't get to judge me on that. I'm allowed to hear an accusation and weigh it and then decide whether it's true based on the evidence or my gut or goddamn tarot cards. And who the hell are you to talk? I saw your face when I told you I wanted to be partners, remember? Wasn't exactly the reaction I'd been hoping for."

"Tony—"

He held up a hand to cut her off, but he'd heard the hint of an apology in her voice and knew that he'd made his point. "I don't think this is about me. I think it's about us."

She cocked her head, wary, but said nothing.

"I think in that moment you realized the same thing I did."

She swallowed. "What's that?"

"That you're not the kind of person who can get tied down. That we felt too much and moved too fast." He dragged his fingers through his hair. Everything he was saying was true—he hated it— but it was true. "I thought I'd go after The Serpent once we left the island. I truly believed that I'd take him out and then, *poof*, I'd have a happy normal life with a steady paycheck, a permanent address, and a woman by my side."

She shifted her weight, but she never stopped looking at him.

"But that's not happening. And what I realized on that island is that I was a fool to ever think it would. I think you realized the same thing. You don't really believe I'm dirty, but you do regret the things we said. So do I." That last part was technically true, but only because he couldn't be with her no matter how he felt. And the real truth was that he felt too goddamn much.

"So you're claiming island fever? The lust of the tropics?"

He heard the edge in her voice and forced himself not to wince. Instead, he walked through the entryway and took a seat on her sofa. When she didn't tell him to get the hell out, he figured that was progress. "I told you how I felt about you, and I meant it." He swallowed as he met her eyes. "This isn't about what I feel. It's about who I am."

She settled into the opposite end of the sofa. "And who's that?"

"Someone who can't add a relationship into the mix. Or a steady job." He cupped his hands behind his neck, trying to ease some of the tension. "I'm not signing on to SSA after all."

Her forehead creased. "Because of me? That's insane. I'm a big girl. And you're not an idiot. Stark Security's a great place for you to land, just like you said. You've made it your mission to kill The Serpent, and once he was dead, you intended to plant some roots. That's what you told me. And now he's dead. So you're welcome."

He grimaced. "I would have liked to have taken that shot, but under the circumstances, I can't really complain."

"And yet you are."

He shook his head. "No. If he weren't dead we'd be having a different conversation."

"Would we?"

What could he say? That if he didn't still have a mission, he'd grab onto her shoulders and tell her that if she wasn't scared of facing a stone-cold killer then she shouldn't be scared of being with him. Because that's what this was about, bottom line. He was certain of it. She'd see a reaction on his face—and why the hell wouldn't he react?—and she'd bolted. Not because she was butt-hurt that a flicker of doubt might enter his mind. Hell, she was better trained than him, and they both knew damn well the first rule in this business was to question everything. To examine everything. To look at the evidence, but not to discount your gut.

And Emma's gut was scared.

But none of that was the point right now. He wasn't staying and they weren't together. So all he said was, "My father's alive, Emma. And until I alter that particular status quo, none of the rest of it matters. Not you, not me, and not Stark Security. I made this my mission a long time ago, and I'm damn sure not going to stop now."

live.
  The word tumbles around in my head, and I can't quite seem to grasp it. To make it real.

Clyde Morgan is alive.

My whole body is hot. Burning. I can practically feel the heft of a gun in my hand. I can almost picture him cowering as I aim. As I fire.

Alive. Is he really alive? How could he have disappeared for so long? And how in the hell am I going to find him?

"Emma?" Tony leans toward me, then lightly touches my knee. "Earth to Emma, are you okay?"

I nod. "Yeah, sorry. I just can't believe he's alive. I mean, the man was blown away when we

were kids. That's what you said, right?" I know it
was. I remember the stories perfectly well. "I
can't believe he could have been alive all this
time and we never knew."

"We?" He repeats. "I didn't think you even
remembered the news from back then."

I nod, remembering that I'd told Tony I didn't
recall hearing the news back when his dad's body
was discovered.

"The royal We," I clarify. "Law enforcement.
The man just went completely under."

"Apparently." His voice is cold. Hard.

I nod, regrouping as I try to figure out what to
do with this new bit of information. This unexpected key that fits into a door to my past.

I stand, then move to the window. I don't
want him to see my face. To see the jumble of
confused emotions underscored by a tug of
uncertainty, both professional and personal.

I'd been so angry—no, *hurt*—when he'd
looked at me that way on the island, but the truth
is that I get it. It wasn't that he didn't trust me,
but that he didn't trust himself. And don't I feel
the same way? Isn't that why I'm so angry?
Because I opened myself up to this man? Trusted
him? And then he hurt my heart?

Except I didn't fully trust him. And now, if I

want in on his search to find Clyde Morgan, I'm going to have to come completely clean.

I've spent my life juggling lies. Holding them close, burying them deep. I'm good at it.

But telling the truth? That's something I suck at.

Now or never, I think, then turn to face him. "So that's why you're turning down the offer to join Stark Security. Because you want to continue this quest. You want to find Clyde Morgan."

He nods.

"Then stay. Join the SSA. The resources are insane. Much better than you could manage on your own."

"Emma—"

"No. Listen. This isn't about what happened between us on the island. I get that you've got tunnel vision for getting this guy. I do, too. And we can nail the fucker a lot faster if we work together—and if we take advantage of the SSA's resources. I mean, you might as well," I add with a shrug. "I'm going to. And you wouldn't want me to beat you to the punch, would you?"

I had to convince him to agree. Yes, it would be awkward working together, but he was right. Focusing on the job was always the best option.

You open your heart, you risk getting hurt. Hadn't he proved that to me during our last night on the island?

"Why are you so fired up to chase down my father?"

And there it was—the question I'd been waiting for. I draw a breath, let it out slowly, then take my seat at the far end of the sofa again. "When I saw your expression on the island, it really did feel like a knife to my gut."

"Come on, Emma. I already told you what was in my head, and I can only explain so many—"

"*No.* Wait. Let me talk." I take a breath and start over. "When I saw your expression I felt sick. I really did. And part of that was because it seemed like you didn't trust me, but the bigger part—" I break off, swallow, and start up again. "The bigger part was that you were right not to."

I keep my eyes on him as I talk, noting the way he leans forward, his brow furrowing.

"We were supposed to be partners on that mission, but I had my own agenda. But now I want to partner with you again. And I owe you more than a half-truth." I shut my eyes, hating that I have to dig into my past and pull it out for examination. But hating more that my silence hurt him.

"Do you remember when I told you that Eliza and I ran because I learned our father was going to sell us?"

"My father? Oh, God, my father was the buyer?"

I nod as he shivers. "I told you I'd never heard of him, but I had. Of course I had. I can't tell you how much I celebrated when I read that he'd been murdered. His body blown apart so much it was practically unrecognizable."

I meet his eyes. "It was staged, of course."

"Yeah." He nods. "Yeah, of course it was. He knew that somehow his predilections had gotten out. He had to disappear. So he staged his death. Probably bribed someone in the LAPD, the coroner's office, who knows. Then he has surgery, changes his appearance, and lives life a little less flamboyantly. Fucking prick."

"How do you know he's alive?" I ask.

"Thea," he says, meeting my eyes. "She told me right before she died."

"Poor kid," I say, pleased to see his sympathetic nod despite the fact that she'd been working for The Serpent.

"She got sucked into a life she didn't want

and couldn't escape." He sighs as he looks at me. "Could have been you. Eliza."

"Don't I know it?"

He reaches for me, pauses, then draws his hand back. "Thanks for telling me all that."

I clench my hand tight, stifling the urge to tug him back and cling to him. Instead, I simply watch as he steeples his hands in front of his face, then exhales. "I'm not joining Stark Security," he says. "I do that and the leads go cold, and I'm stuck getting shuttled off to the far side of the globe on some other mission. I did that when I was working for Deliverance, and that was fine because most of the time The Serpent had gone under. But now that I know my father is alive? I'm not going to rest until he's dead."

"But the resources are—"

"I'm saying no to joining. I'm not saying no to you."

My heart does a little tripping number, even though I know perfectly well he's not talking about us personally. "Explain."

"*You* push the mission. Tell Stark and Ryan what Morgan means to you. Tell Quince and Eliza, too," he adds, and I nod. It's time my sister knew, anyway. "And then you tell him about the connection. And we team up. Like a joint task force. I get the benefit of Stark Security without the ties. You get a pretty damn awesome partner."

"True," I laugh. "But I don't get you."

The words are out before I realize I've said them, and I immediately scramble to cover the gaff. "I don't mean hearts and flowers and happy ever afters," I say. "I just mean that we had a good time on the island."

"We did," he says, then frowns. "Is that what you want? An island-style arrangement? Friends-with-benefits?"

Part of me wants to jump at the chance. I miss his touch. I miss having him right beside me. The scent of him when he's close to me. I can't even remember the last time I turned down a FWB deal with someone I was attracted to, but this time there's not even a temptation. Because the truth is that I want more. I've never wanted it before. I'm not sure if I'll ever want it again.

But I'm not about to say it out loud because I know it's not what he needs. He needs freedom. He needs his vendetta. And until his father is either dead or this hot core inside him burns out, he won't stay. And he sure as hell wouldn't ever be mine.

—————

"I'm not saying no," Ryan Hunter says from where he sits behind his desk facing Tony and me. "I just want you to lay it all out for me. I want a sense of how long you'll be unavailable," he adds, his eyes on me. "And I want an idea of how long we'll have to convince Mr. Santos to join up permanently."

"I'm not opposed to the idea," Tony says. "But until I've found him, I stay a free agent, and this mission occupies one hundred percent of my time. Whether it takes ten minutes or ten years."

"Understood."

"You also need to understand that I'm not playing a catch and call the cops game here. You know what he did to me. To my family." He nods toward me. "You know what Eliza and Emma almost got sucked into. And who knows how many girls didn't escape that predatory bastard."

"I know."

"Do you? Because I want to be crystal clear. I find him, I'm killing him. There is no other end to this mission."

"As this isn't to be an SSA mission, I wouldn't presume to make that call. We are, however, happy to offer you the use of some SSA resources, as well as agent Tucker's time and skill. At least for a limited period. How you run the mission in that period is your call."

He speaks with stiff formality, but I hear the smile in his voice, especially when he says, "Welcome to the SSA, Santos. Even if only as our guest."

Beside me, Tony grins "Happy to be here. I'll be even happier if I can make some progress. "

"You're planning on starting with Dailey?" Ryan asks. Referring to the man who, supposedly, took over Morgan's business.

"Emma and I ran through the options last night," he says. "We're going to throw out multiple wads and see what sticks. Dailey's the priority. If we can track down a location or an associate, that could be a huge lead."

"But we're also going to follow the money," I chime in. "Morgan will have set up a trust that funded the continuation of his businesses."

"I never followed the money because I believed my father to be dead. But now..."

Ryan nods. "Now, he's paying for his living expenses somehow."

"Exactly," Tony says.

"Other angles?" Ryan asks.

"The girl," I say. "She worked for Dailey, so

there's a connection. She apparently slept with The Serpent, so that's another. And she knew that Clyde Morgan is still alive."

"Presumably," Ryan says, and Tony and I both have to nod. That's something else we discussed last night. Thea may have it completely wrong. Or we might have misread her completely, and instead of being an innocent, she was as vile as The Serpent and just wanted to mess with Tony's head.

"All right," Ryan says. "Those are three solid angles. I think you two are off to a good start." He turns his attention to Tony. "Whatever resources you need, you just ask. And as for running the searches, so long as you don't take time away from their regular assignments, feel free to pull Mario or Denny in for whatever you need. You won't find two better techs this side of Texas." He grins, and I know that he's thinking of Noah Carter, another guy who used to be part of Deliverance, but now works for Stark Applied Technology. When I see Tony grin, I know that he's gotten the reference as well.

"We intend to make you like it here," Ryan continues, "To feel like you're part of the team. So you'll want to stay."

Tony nods, then casts a quick glance toward

me. "It wouldn't take much convincing," he says, and I'm certain that the heat I hear in his voice isn't my imagination. "But Morgan's my priority. Everything else comes second."

I feel an unwelcome twist in my chest. I don't want to react so viscerally to this man, especially since I know that's the way it has to be. And, honestly, if I were in his shoes, I'd feel the same.

We wrap up with Ryan, then step out of his office and into the Stark Security bullpen. It's filled with over a dozen desks, some assigned to an agent, some open for anybody who needs some extra space, or for guests like Tony.

As I glance around, looking for an empty space that Tony can commandeer, I see Liam and Quince walk through the door. I nudge Tony, then nod in their direction. "Why don't you go grab Liam," I suggest. "Tell him you're a semi-agent here now."

"Funny."

"Well, it's true. And you know he's going to try to convince you to make it a permanent thing."

"It's not convincing I need," he says.

"It's closure. I know. But even so. Go talk to him. He can introduce you to Mario and Denny.

I assume he already knows a significant amount about what you're doing?"

"Not all of it, but some. We became pretty good friends during our tenure at Deliverance." He cocks his head, one brow lifting as he studies me. "You tired of me so soon? Regretting this new found partnership?"

I roll my eyes. "I have something personal I need to talk to Quince about."

"Is this personal having to do with your sister?"

"No comment."

He flashes me a knowing smile, then starts walking in that direction, calling out for Liam, who spreads his arms and flashes a bright smile. "Tony, my man, I'm so glad you're here. What's up?"

As Tony starts to explain to Liam what he needs, I make a beeline for Quince. "Whatcha got in your pocket?" I ask with a tease in my voice. "I'm guessing there's still a ring rattling around with your change and car keys."

"Emma..."

"Because I haven't gotten a squealing, giddy call from my sister to tell me that she's engaged to the love of her life." I narrow my eyes. "And the love of her life told me that he was proposing soon."

"Your worse than a mother on one of those horrible old American sitcoms."

"Guilty. When are you making an honest woman of her?"

"To think I'll have you as an in-law one day..." He trails off with a wink, then hurries on when I cock my head and cross my arms. "I've been planning the perfect evening. I just made a reservation. You're not going to blow this for me, are you?"

"I would never do that." I look him up and down. "Unless you're not man enough to get it done yourself."

He rolls his eyes. "I love your sister. It's a shame I have to get the baggage, too."

I laugh. "Love you, too, brother-to-be."

A hint of color rises on his cheeks, and I almost regret ribbing him. *Almost*. I've grown to love this man like a brother. And the sooner he makes my sister happy—correction, *happier*—the better.

Honestly, I'm not entirely sure where this pressure to push their engagement along is coming from. Then I see Tony and Liam bent over Mario's computer, and I have to admit that I might have a clue.

The pressure's stemming from happiness. The need to grab it. Claim it.

And if I can't have my personal shot, then at the very least I want Eliza to have enough for both of us.

CHAPTER TWENTY-ONE

I'll say one thing about working in covert ops—there's not a lot of downtime. Granted, I was never the person responsible for finding the bad guy. Instead, I was the person who took the file I was given, then used the information to either grab the bad guy and bring him in for interrogation or just rid the world of him entirely.

In other words, I'm used to action.

Granted, I spent a lot of years working as a private investigator, but many of those years were just a cover for my covert work for the SOC. But there were still days that I had to spend trolling through credit reports and old newspaper clippings while my eyes burned from staring at a computer monitor. Or, worse, long nights parked outside someone's house with a camera, thermos of coffee, and no place to pee. Those jobs were the worst, and definitely the low point of my PI career.

I'll say this for the SSA—it has sparkling bathroom facilities, super speedy computers, an amazing break room, and a snack bar that probably puts the most doting grandmother to shame. So I'm counting this career shift as a step up.

Even so, after two days of slogging through documents and print outs, theories and dead-ends, I'm getting so antsy I'm ready to ask Ryan if there's someone—*anyone*—he needs tracked down on another matter. Because I will happily go out into the world and drag the SOB back by the scruff of his neck.

"You look ready to stab someone with a fork."

I tilt my head up to find Tony grinning down at me, the echo of that low, sexy voice lingering in my mind. I force myself not to smile and instead offer him my best scowl. "You're not wrong. Careful I don't target you."

He laughs, then comes around to my side of the desk and leans against it. He's barely five inches away now, and I wish he'd edge away a bit more. Just a few more inches so that I can't smell the spice of his cologne, a scent that's tangling me up inside.

For the last forty-eight hours, I've been having a hell of a time focusing on my work. How can I when he's sitting just two desks over? And though I tell myself not to be adolescent, whenever I finish a task and take a break, I find myself sneaking looks at him.

And the thing that's the most frustrating? On at least half of those looks, he's sneaking one right back.

The last time—less than an hour ago before I escaped to grab a croissant from the snack bar— I'd held his gaze. I said nothing, but I didn't look away. I want him. I do. And, yes, I get why he's holding back. I understand it. If it were me, I'd probably do the same. God knows I've put myself and my jobs ahead of every other person I've ever slept with.

But therein lies the rub. Because for reasons I don't understand, Tony is in a category all his own. And, dammit, I'm just enough of an asshole not to make this easy on him.

So, yeah. Maybe I want to stab him with that fork.

"You want to tell me why you're here?" I don't mean to snap, but it comes out that way.

He holds up his hands in surrender. "Just checking in."

"No. You were—*shit*." I shove back my chair, then cock my head. "With me."

I don't check to make sure he's following. I just storm across the room and then out the glass door that opens onto a charming outdoor sitting area that the SSA shares with other tenants in the Domino, a Santa Monica business complex owned by Stark and his half-brother, architect Jackson Steele.

"What the hell are you doing?" I demand as soon as we're through the door and around a corner so as to not be on display for everyone at the SSA to see.

"I was going to ask how your research is going. But you looked to be so irritated I changed gears. You want to tell me why you're biting my head off?"

"I'm not—shit. Yes, I am. Damn." I plop my ass down on one of the stone benches. "I'm sorry. This is on me. It's just that—dammit, Tony, there's a thing between us. A connection. And I know you feel it too, because I catch you looking at me, and it's there."

"What is?"

"I don't know. A glimmer. A heat. It's the

thing between us, and it's there. Am I insane? Do you really not see it? Is this all one-sided? Because tell me if it is and I'll back off faster than you can say Temporary Restraining Order."

He doesn't laugh. On the contrary, he looks a little miserable. "No. It's not one-sided."

"Then why are we ignoring it?"

"To make it easier," he says, and I burst out laughing. To his credit, he laughs, too, then drags his fingers through his hair, rumpling it so that it looks a bit like it does after sex.

I resist the urge to smooth it back down and concentrate on slowing my pulse.

"Look," he finally says. "I'm not ignoring it. But I'm also not acting on it. I don't know. Maybe I should never have parked this investigation at Stark Security."

Now I feel like a heel. "No. You've been playing the lone wolf for long enough. You need the support. Manpower and hardware. This isn't on you. It's on me. I'm not like this. Not ever. You just..." I trail off with a shrug.

"What?"

"You were—well, you were unexpected."

He nods slowly and we share a small smile. "Yeah, well, so were you."

I sigh, wishing this were easier. But I really

do understand. He's made it clear that unless and until this case closes, he doesn't want a relationship. And he doesn't want to just be fuck buddies.

And for the first time, I don't want that either. Not with him. With Tony, that would be like a slap in the face. Where Tony is concerned, I want the real deal or nothing.

I'm more frustrated with myself than I am with the situation. It's not as if we were high school sweethearts ripped apart after years of dating. This whole thing is all brand new, and yet I've never felt like this before. And I know myself well enough to know that it's real. And the not having him is driving me crazy. But I'm not going to push. I couldn't live with myself if he caved because I pushed.

All of which is why I'm a mess. And why I'm having a hell of a time focusing at work whenever he's around.

Then again, maybe Tony's not really to blame on that front. Maybe it's because we don't seem to be getting anywhere. Thea, Dailey, Morgan. These are all people who seem to live off the grid. Because after two days of searching, the crack team at the Stark Security Agency is still mining. So far, none of us have struck gold.

"Any luck on the plastic surgery end?" I ask Tony, who's been following the theory that for Morgan to disappear, he had to have a new appearance. And someone had to give it to him.

"I've got a lead on a doctor in Costa Rica who may have worked on him," he says. "Waiting on some follow-up. How about you? Has Lorenzo gotten back to you about Thea?"

My former PI partner is a retired cop and one of the best at tracking people I've ever met, even people whose primary residence was an abandoned car or trash-strewn doorstep.

"Not yet. I was hoping to hear—"

The sharp chime of my phone interrupts me, and we both glance down at the name on the display. *Lorenzo.*

I meet Tony's eyes, and he holds up crossed fingers. I'm grinning when I put the phone on speaker. "I've got Tony on the line, too," I say right off the bat, because Eliza had told him a bit about Tony, and he'd called to give me a fatherly pep talk that basically came down to the fact that I needed to quit screwing around—literally—and settle down. And if my sister liked this guy, he must be a good one.

With anyone else, I would have told them to fuck off. But Lorenzo's as close to a dad as I've ever had, and his paternal opinions are as much a part of him as his gruffness.

"What have you got for us?"

"She's a tough one, but the puzzle's startin' to come together. I found an address from four years ago, but she's long gone from there. But I can confirm her name. Theadora Dempsey. Goes by Thea. I managed to track down her agent from when she was trying to be an actress. That led me to a restaurant in Studio City where she used to wait tables, and the dishwasher there remembered her, and—"

"Lorenzo, I already know you're amazing at this, but can you cut to the chase? Did she lead you to Dailey or Morgan?"

I hear him huff, and watch as Tony grins. "I'm getting there, aren't I? I don't have a specific address, not for her, not for her workplace. But I did get some hits on her credit card that are interesting. Girl drove a little Fiat. Filled it up about once a week. And always at a Chevron in Brentwood. I just texted you the address. I figure she's either got a boyfriend or a job. And since most of the charges were in the morning before nine, I'm thinking job."

"Lorenzo, it's Tony. You're a bad ass investigator, my man."

"You think I don't know it? You two owe me a pizza. You know what I like, young lady."

"I'm ordering as soon as we hang up."

"I'll call if I get more. Give your sister a hug from me."

"Miss you, too, and I will. Later," I say, and end the call.

When I look up, Tony's smiling at me.

"What?" I demand as I text the Chevron address to Denny, then send in the order for delivery to Lorenzo's office, which doubles as his house these days. I use Flying Saucer Pizza so often that they just keep my credit card on file. I glance back up at Tony, who hasn't answered, and roll my hand in an effort to get him to answer.

"I just like him, that's all. And I like that he's been there for you and Eliza."

"He was a good cop, he's a great PI, and he's the best man I know. Though you rank high on my list," I admit, even though I'm probably crossing a non-relationship line.

But all Tony says is, "Thanks. That means a lot."

His eyes are fixed on me as he says it, and I feel the crackle in the air. The dangerous kind, like the way the air feels before lightning strikes.

For a moment, we both just stand there. Then he clears his throat, and I sag a bit, though I'm not sure if it's in relief or disappointment.

I glance over and notice that Quince is looking at me through the glass door, his brow furrowed. I turn away quickly, not even wanting to know what he's thinking about, only to realize that Tony's been speaking and I haven't heard a word.

"What?"

"I said pizza sounds like a great idea. Why don't you order a dozen or so large for the office. A variety of toppings. My treat, since everyone's working late. And with this Chevron intel, I have a feeling we'll be working even later."

"That's a great idea. Very sweet."

"Just feeding the troops," he says as we head back inside, but I know it's more than that. When Ryan first agreed to let us bring Tony's mission to the SSA, Tony was an outsider. Now he's full-on part of the team. More than that, for this job, he's the leader. And a leader takes care of his people.

"Oh, fuck me."

The curse comes from Denny's workstation, and I frown, thinking that she's annoyed we're working late. Her husband, Mason, is still on official leave as he continues a massive debriefing with the SOC. I didn't work with him there, but I know the story, and the idea of daily meetings to try to pull out bits and pieces of memory sounds horrible to me. Mason, however, assured me that it's not. "Best thing ever," he'd said. "Every day, I remember a little bit more about Denny. It's like Christmas all over again."

It's a nice sentiment, but I still think the process would drive me bonkers. Then again, after all Mason went through, maybe he's decided that the only way to live life is to look at the upside.

I glance at Tony and sigh. Maybe I should take a page from Mason's book, and instead of moping that I don't have everything I want from this man, I should be grateful for what we did have. If it weren't for Tony, I'm not sure I'd ever have felt like this. And even though this part is painful as hell, what we shared has been wonderful. Maybe that's supposed to be enough. Maybe for some people, it would be.

I'm just not sure I'm one of those people.

"Guys!" Denny's call rings out. "Did you not hear me? Get over here."

I catch both Quincy and Tony's eyes, and we

hurry over. Liam's already there, and Mario rolls over, his desk chair coming to a perfect stop beside Liam, whose rock-solid build dwarfs Mario's skinny ass.

"Sorry. Didn't realize the curse was a battle cry," Quincy says, and Denny shoots him a killer glare that doesn't even faze him. They often work as partners, so I suppose he's used to her withering looks.

"I have no idea how yesterday's search didn't pull this, but look."

She pushes a lock of blond hair out of her face as she points to her screen, and we all bend forward.

"The Daily Meditation Foundation." I read the title on the file aloud. "Maybe I'm too tired, but I don't get it."

"It's one of the entities created from Morgan's trust. And it's just the kind of thing I was looking for, so why it didn't get pulled in the first batch, I really—never mind. Moving on. The point is the name. Daily. *Dailey*. Get it?"

"You think this entity is somehow a cover for Harvey Dailey?"

She looks back over her shoulder at us. "I think right now it's the best lead we have."

"Do you have an address?" Tony asks.

"That's the beauty of it," Denny says. "It popped when I was cross-referencing a two mile radius around your Chevron station. I don't know if it's your answer," she says, "but at least it's a lead."

CHAPTER TWENTY-TWO

The Dailey Meditation Foundation was a solid lead, but it was useless without an address. And that took a bit more time. The corporate documents that Denny had located had been filed with the state over a year ago, and the address listed was simply a PO Box in a strip shopping center by the Chevron.

Now Denny was working her magic to track down a current physical address, and Tony was pacing impatiently behind her.

"Haven't you ever heard of watched pots?" She swiveled in her chair and scowled at him. "Go get a coffee or something. For that matter, go get one for me."

Since keeping her caffeinated seemed to be one of the most useful things he could do at that point, Tony nodded, then set off toward the break room. As he did, Emma fell in step beside him.

"You hanging in there?" she asked, as Tony waited for the coffee machine to work its magic.

"I'm ready to get moving," Tony said. "I've never been this close before—which is ironic, since for all I know, I'm not even close at all."

"I think you are," she said. "It feels ... buzzy."

He laughed. It was a ridiculous way to describe that familiar feeling. The sense of being right at the end of a mission when everything pulled together. Ridiculous, but also completely accurate. "Yeah," he agreed. "It does."

He drew in a breath, wanting to say more, but not sure if he should. Then he thought, fuck it. If it was the wrong thing to say, then so be it. He'd been an ass enough times in his life to know he'd survive doing it one more time.

"Emma?"

She'd turned, and was about to open the refrigerator. Now, she looked over her shoulder. For just a moment, he thought he saw hope in her eyes, but then it disappeared, and he saw only a bland query? "Yeah?"

"I really hope we're close. I really hope this is the end."

The muscles in her face tightened, and she

shook her head sadly. "Don't, okay? I understand your reasoning, but all you're doing is drawing a line in the sand. But guess what, Tony, you're the one holding the stick. You can draw that line anywhere you want it. So don't pretend like it's closing the case that marks the line. You've got the power to move it anywhere you damn well please."

She shrugged, as if she'd just said the most basic thing in the world, then walked away without bothering to get anything out of the fridge. He watched her go, knowing she was right, but not sure he had the strength to either move the line or to stop the constant motion of the waves.

Fortunately, he didn't have to keep his lines, his motives, or his personal roadblocks for much longer, because by the time he returned with Denny's coffee, she'd tracked down the address.

The Daily Meditation Foundation was located in a gated, three-story private residence on two acres in Brentwood, a fact that matched up well with what they knew of Thea's movements. Tony considered moving on the intel right away, but he was too well trained to risk the success of a mission by moving in too quickly.

Instead, he ordered five rotating teams to

watch the place for a full, and painfully long, forty-eight hours with the goal of assessing who was coming and going, and at what times.

It was perhaps the longest two days of his life, but when it ended, they'd learned that the residence rarely had visitors, and that Harvey Dailey did in fact reside on the premises.

He and Emma had been on shift when Dailey emerged from the gate for a walk around the block. Skinny and frail in his mid-seventies, with white hair that stood out in tufts, he sported a handlebar mustache and looked like he should be starring in spoofs of old westerns.

As they had no description of Dailey, they hadn't known for certain that's who the old man was when they first saw him. They'd captured an image and sent it to Denny, but nothing had popped on the facial recognition database, though she pointed out that a facial search could sometimes take days for results.

The thought of waiting days was enough to make Tony want to throw up his hands and just propose that they enter the residence without confirmation.

Fortunately, they were able to get positive ID when a neighbor joined the man on the sidewalk, calling him by name as they started up a conversation.

"So now we know," Tony said. They were about half a block down the road, and he'd been watching the scene through binoculars, adept enough at lip reading to confirm the name.

In the passenger seat, Emma nodded, but there was a little V above her nose, as he'd noticed there often when she was thinking.

"All right," he said. "What's the problem?"

She shook her head. "Nothing solid. He doesn't seem the type. And there's something off about the entire situation that I can't put my finger on."

Tony nodded. He'd felt it, too. "I don't see this guy in bed with The Serpent or my father. But at the same time, I've taken down a lot of bad asses, and I promise you, not all of them look like hardened criminals. There's plenty of murderous pricks who look like your favorite grandpa."

"I never knew my grandpa," Emma said, "but I know what you're saying. And I still think that something feels off."

"He might be a pawn. It's possible someone is just using his name for a front operation. But we've ID-ed him as a Harvey Dailey. We know that Thea was working for a Harvey Dailey. And we know that this house belongs to a foundation held in the name of Harvey Dailey. At this point I don't think we have any choice but to go in and figure out what's what."

"Fair enough. Let's go report back and spec out a mission plan."

They drove back in silence, and he was certain she was being quiet as a courtesy, assuming that he was deep in thought about how to handle the mission. In fact, that wasn't the case. He trusted her instincts, and her concerns about this man gave him pause. Could Dailey be an innocent in all of this?

At the end of the day, for the purposes of this mission, it didn't matter. There was no way he'd forgo entering that property to have a look around. He needed to know if the Dailey Meditation Foundation held any documentation about Clyde Morgan or The Serpent. The latter was dead, but details like The Serpent's real name might lead back to Morgan.

The connection between Dailey and Morgan was the only solid lead he had, and he was determined to pursue it. This was more than just a mission, after all. It was his life. And he damn well wanted closure.

Worst case, Dailey knew nothing and was a

pawn. Best case, Dailey knew everything and could draw him a map.

And if Dailey wouldn't talk? Well, there was always Quincy. His unique skill set had been honed in British Intelligence. If Quincy couldn't get answers, there were no answer to be had.

When they reached the SSA, they walked in on what seemed like a buzzing bee hive with significantly more noise and activity than was usual for the bullpen. At first, Tony thought there'd been a break in the case—but he dismissed that possibility. Someone would have texted him right away.

Perhaps something in one of the other operations?

He was about to signal Mario over when the crowd parted and he got a glimpse of Eliza standing next to Quincy with her left hand extended, a diamond ring sparkling so brightly that he could see its shine from halfway across the room, not to mention the glow of Eliza herself.

Beside him, Emma squealed, flashed him a huge smile that made his heart race, then ran forward to embrace her sister. "Oh my God, you got engaged last night and you didn't call me?"

She shot an annoyed look at Quince who held up his hands in a gesture of self-defense.

"It didn't exactly go according to plan," Quincy said.

"I was doing the laundry," Eliza said, her voice sheepish. "I decided to wash his pants. I'll never do that again without permission."

"Oh my God," Emma said, and Tony assumed she knew more about the state of Quince's pants than Tony did. "You found the ring."

"You knew?"

"He told me," Emma said. "I asked when he was going to make an honest woman of you. I think there was a dinner involved."

"We still did the dinner," Eliza said, still beaming. She turned back to Quincy. "I'm so sorry I spoiled it."

"Are you daft, love? You said yes, didn't you?" Quincy was grinning so broadly that Tony was certain his facial muscles were going to ache tomorrow morning. But at the same time, Tony couldn't deny that he'd be happy to feel that ache himself someday. It was a shocking revelation, but true. He'd never thought of marriage before. And he knew damn well that it wasn't simply

Quince and Eliza's engagement that had it sneaking into his head now.

From across the crowd, Quince caught his eye. Then he winked and glanced toward Emma.

Tony shook his head as if exasperated, then rolled his eyes just for effect. But the truth was, he wasn't exasperated at all. In fact, he was thinking about joy. About love.

Most of all, for the first time that he could remember, he was thinking about a future.

———

Quince and Liam entered first, breaching the first level and taking care of cutting the security feed. Tony and Emma scaled the building and entered from the third floor balcony. Denny was monitoring in the control van, with Mario and another agent that Tony hadn't met—Trevor—assisting.

Two other Stark Security agents, Winston and Leah, weren't on the operation at all. They'd been called out of town the day before with a hot lead on one of their active investigations.

"All clear in the living room." Quince's voice came clearly through Tony's earpiece. "Moving to the kitchen."

"Entry hall and master bedroom clear," Liam said. "Moving down the hall."

On the third floor, Emma was already inside as Tony waited on the balcony, checking the yard for any sign that they'd been detected. He saw nothing, and when he turned back, Emma signaled to him that the room was all clear, too.

He entered as she slowly opened the door to exit the bedroom. They didn't expect to find anyone in the house. They'd used heat sensing technology to scan the place, and there'd been no signs of anybody on the premises. Still, procedure existed for a reason. Better to follow it than make a mistake.

As they moved through the house, both teams continued to check in. Below them, Quince and Liam did the same.

"First floor secure," Quince stated. "Moving up to the second."

"Finishing our reconnaissance now," Emma said. "Only the office left to go." She looked over her shoulder at Tony, who was still down the hall. He nodded for her to go ahead and enter the final room. She did, took a step in, and froze, her back going stiff.

"We have a DB," she said. "Repeat, we have a DB."

He hurried to her side, taking care to scan for any trouble on the way, and when he reached the office, he saw what she did. Harvey Dailey sitting behind his desk chair, a bullet to the brain.

"He's been there a while," she said, and Tony nodded.

"Probably killed not long after we saw him. He was cold when we ran the heat scan, that's for sure."

"On our way," Quince said, his voice filling Tony's ear.

"Negative," Emma said. "Secure the second floor. We have this under control."

She looked at Tony, "This doesn't make any sense. It can't be a coincidence."

"No," he agreed. "Someone knew we were coming. And that someone didn't want us to talk to him."

"But that doesn't make any sense. Dailey only landed on your radar because of Thea—and she's dead. And the only person who might have cause to know that she'd tell you about Dailey would be The Serpent, and I killed him."

"Yes, Thea's dead," Tony said, "but it's possible someone identified me while we were on the island."

"You're thinking that since Thea worked for

Dailey there may be some other player who assumes that you'll make the connection and follow the path back here."

He nodded. "I suppose this confirms our suspicions about Dailey. But we still don't know what information Dailey has."

She lifted a shoulder. "And that's why we're going to be spending the next few hours going through his filing cabinets. And we should get Denny or Mario in here to hack his computer."

He nodded and tapped his earpiece, relaying the command to come to the office to the rest of the team.

"Here's another interesting tidbit to throw into the mix," Denny said, her voice tinny in his ear. "I've been going through the records, trying to figure out why I missed that document the first time. It wasn't uploaded into the Secretary of State's records until about twenty minutes before I downloaded it."

Emma and Tony looked at each other. He could see the moment she understood, just as he did.

"Oh, Christ. It's a setup," Denny said, obviously on the same wavelength they were. "Get the fuck out of there."

They'd already started to move, but it was too

late. He heard the creak of the floorboard, and turned just in time to see one of the wooden wall panels open, revealing not only a camouflaged hidey-hole, but also a familiar man dressed in a full-body skin suit—the kind designed to hide from heat-sensing technology. And he's holding a pistol in his hand.

The Serpent.

He didn't have the shot yet, though, and as he shifted his aim, Tony launched himself, tackling Emma to the ground at the same time the shot rang out.

It was followed immediately by another, and from his position on top of Emma, Tony saw The Serpent's leg collapse under him. He fell, knocked down by the force of the bullet to his thigh and, undoubtedly, the searing pain of the injury.

Liam sprinted to him, the weapon he'd just fired still held at the ready. He kicked The Serpent's firearm away, then held the not-dead-after-all man at bay with the point of his gun.

Quince appeared in the doorway next, also armed and ready. Immediately, he assessed the situation, then offered Tony and Emma a hand up.

He aimed his chin toward The Serpent, then

looked back at Tony with a casual shrug. "To be honest, I'd rather just kill the fucker. But we should probably take him back to the office and let me have a go at him." He flashed a dangerous smile that had the man on the floor cringing. "We'll have a little party, you and me. And you can tell me every one of your goddamn bloody secrets."

CHAPTER TWENTY-THREE

I pace in front of the one-way glass, watching Quincy as he sits in front of The Serpent. His leg is now bandaged, and from what Colonel Anderson Seagrave tells me, The Serpent's not feeling any pain. On top of the drugs the SSA medic gave him before stitching up the wound, Quincy has filled him with a proprietary pharmaceutical array that not only eases the pain in his leg, but also makes him more willing to share all of his secrets.

I glanced down at Seagrave who's idly moving his wheelchair back and forth as he watches the show going on behind the glass. He's in his mid-forties with dark hair going gray at the temples and an easy smile that doesn't detract from his commanding presence. We worked together for a long time, and though we butted heads often, I have nothing but respect for him.

"How long does this usually take?" I ask.

Behind me, Tony is pacing. "It's never a fast process," he says. "The stronger the subject, the longer it takes. Considering what we know about The Serpent, it might take forever."

"Under the circumstances, I'm willing to wait forever."

"Right now, Quince is working to obtain information about your father," Seagrave says looking at Tony. "After that, he can take a break. We'll take your new friend back to the SOC. Let our people work on him. You both did amazing work, by the way. Truly amazing."

Tony shrugs, and I'm certain I know what he's thinking. Seagrave doesn't have to butter him up. Once he knows about his father, he doesn't really care what happens to The Serpent.

I care though. Because The Serpent knows about Winston's past, and I care about my friend.

I texted Winston an hour ago, letting him know that The Serpent is in our custody. He's out of the state right now, but I know he's going to be interested in what's in the bastard's head. Maybe it'll even bring him some closure.

I doubt it though.

I walk over to Tony then reach for his hand. I pull back at the last minute, afraid that if I make the connection, I won't ever want to break it again. "How are you holding up?"

"I'm hanging in there. I can't believe we're this close to the end. Feels like time has started moving more slowly."

"We're getting closer," I assure him. "Eventually Quincy will find out about your father."

Tony nods. "I know. I spent years working with that man. If Quincy can't find out where my father is, then my father doesn't exist on this planet."

He flashes me a smile, and I feel a bit of relief flow through me. I can't imagine how hard this is on him, knowing that his father has been alive all this time when the only thing he ever wanted to do was make the son-of-a-bitch pay for destroying Tony's family and childhood.

He looks at me, then reaches out and tucks a lock of my hair behind my ear. It's a casual gesture, but intimate at the same time. I feel the shiver of connection run through me.

Exactly what I didn't want to feel. Exactly what I want.

And I tell myself that this is not the time or the place for these emotions. Right now, this is about Tony and his father and what's happening in that interrogation room.

"Do you want to be on the team when we go after my father?" Tony asks.

I feel my eyes go wide with surprise. "Hell, yes."

I see a hint of a smile touch his lips. "We agree that I'm the one leading the team?"

"Honestly, I think you're too emotionally involved. But I also know you'll throw a tantrum if you don't lead it."

He chuckles. "Damn right I will." He looks me up and down. "You're exhausted."

"You look pretty sharp and spiffy yourself."

"I mean it. You're completely drained. And I know I am too. If you want to be on the team, I need you sharp. I need you rested. I need me rested too."

"Fine." I look at him. "I'm going to my place to take a nap. I have a guest bedroom. Do you want to come with me, or shall we meet back here later?"

He hesitates before answering, then says, "A guest bedroom sounds perfect."

We're in my living room in under fifteen minutes. And once again, I want to touch him.

To tell him that this will all be okay. To let him know that I believe it will soon be over.

And to reassure him that that I'm there for whatever he needs.

As for what I need...

I need the feel of his arms around me. I need to feel his body against mine. I need this to be over so that I can have this man again.

But I have to be realistic, too. I know that it might never be over. The Serpent might not know where Clyde Morgan is. Or if he does know, Morgan may well have moved on. There's no certainty in this business. As I'm fast learning, there's no certainty in relationships either.

I don't say any of that, of course. Instead, I just point Tony toward the guest bedroom and ask him one simple question. "You'll wake me if Quince calls?"

"Of course."

I nod. "Okay then. I'll see you when he calls or when we both wake up. Whichever comes first."

I don't bother changing clothes. I'm too wiped. All I do is kick off my shoes, then pull back the duvet and slide under. I think I'm asleep before my head even hits the pillow, but I come wide awake, the moment I feel the mattress shift.

"It's okay. It's me." I feel his hand on my hip at the same time as he speaks, and I relax into my pillow.

"Holy Christ. You realize I keep a gun in that drawer. You could be dead by now."

"I don't think so. You're far too good to shoot without knowing who you're shooting."

"Maybe I was going to shoot you for waking me up," I retort. "I barely got to sleep."

I prop myself up on an elbow and try to blink away the cobwebs. "Did we hear from Quince?"

He shakes his head. "No. Not yet."

I frown, suddenly concerned. "What's wrong?" I push myself all the way up so that my back is against the headboard. "Tony, tell me what's going on."

"We need to talk."

My stomach twists at the measured and unfamiliar tone in his voice. "Oh." I really don't know what else to say.

"This isn't working for me." He scrubs his hands over his face and looks at me. "I'm so sorry."

"Oh." I say again. I feel sick. And I don't understand how he can be breaking up with me a second time when we're not even together right now.

"I could have died in Dailey's office. You could have, too. Thank God you were there to save me, but we could have died. We survived on pure luck."

"That's not true, and you know it. We survived because of training. Sharp instincts. Fast reactions."

"Maybe. Maybe not. Doesn't matter." He draws in a breath, then lets it out slowly. "The point is I don't want to wait until I don't have a mission. There will always be a mission."

I frown, trying to put his words in the context of where I thought this conversation was going. But like a piece of a puzzle that belongs to a different picture entirely, nothing fits at all.

"I don't know if I'll find my dad tomorrow or the next day or ever. Maybe I'll keep looking and maybe I won't. Maybe I find him, maybe I don't. But the bottom line is that I already found you."

He brushes my cheek as I try not to let the hope that has started as a trickle turn into a massive flood.

"I want you there with me. I want you by my side, Emma. I want to sign on at Stark Security. I want a partner, sweetheart, and not just for work."

I stare at him, my heart filling so that my

chest feels as though it might burst. I want to say all the pretty words back to him. Words of love and passion and hope and the future. But I have no idea what words to say. All I have are these feelings in my heart.

I guess that's okay, though, because he seems to have plenty of words.

"I've fallen in love with you Emma," he says, taking my breath away. "I've spent my whole life chasing a goddamn vendetta, thinking that coming to the end of it would make me whole. But that's not the answer."

He takes my hands and the warmth of his touch flows through me like an elixir, bringing me fully back to life. "It's you, Emma. You're the answer. You're what makes me whole."

"Wow," I say. "Tony, I—"

I'm still struggling for words, so I say the only thing that comes into my mind. The only thing that's flashing in there like neon. "I've fallen in love with you, too."

He looks at me, and for a moment I can't read his expression. Then I see the fire in his eyes. And before I can say or do anything else, he pulls me close and captures my mouth with his.

I melt against him, so happy that this man belongs to me that I want to cry. That's not who I am, though. I'm not a woman who gets emotional. I'm not a woman who ever thought she needed anybody except her sister.

But there's no denying that I need this man.

I wrap my arms around his neck and cling to him, almost afraid that if I let go, he'll disappear and this will all be a dream.

But that's not me either. I'm not a girl who avoids reality. I'm not a woman who's afraid to look at the hard questions. And so I slowly pull back to cup his face in my hands. "Are you sure? Because honestly, Tony, if you walk away ... if you change your mind ... I don't think I'll be able to survive."

"You would," he says. "You're the strongest person I know. But it won't ever be an issue, because I'm not leaving."

"Good. Because no matter what, I'm stronger with you."

"You're all I want," he says. "All I need. I've been chasing shadows. I know that. What I should've been chasing was love. Baby, please. Please know that I love you."

I take his hand and I press it to my heart. "I've never been one for sentiment," I say, " but I do know it."

I take his hand and press it to my lips. "Would you do something for me?"

"Anything."

"Would you make love to me?"

His smile is slow and deliciously wicked. "With pleasure."

CHAPTER TWENTY-FOUR

Tony moved slowly inside her, their eyes locked on each other. Her lips were parted, and her face was alight with pleasure. With love.

Even if he lived for a thousand years, he knew damn well that he would never understand what he did to deserve this woman. This strong, beautiful woman who loved him so openly and so completely.

She was his other half, and it was a miracle that somehow through all the shit of their lives, they managed to come together.

"Hey," she said, a sensual smile playing on those beautiful lips. "Where are you?"

"Here. With you. Always."

"Good answer." She wiggled her hips. "But I was wondering where your mind had gone."

"I was thinking about you. I was thinking about how much I love you. What a miracle you are to me."

"What *we* are to each other, you mean. Such a short amount of time in the calendar of my life, but now I can't even imagine a life without you. How weird is that?"

"If you're weird, I am, too. Because I can't imagine life without you."

She laughed. "Are we becoming sappy? I don't think that's part of my job spec. I'm supposed to be a hard ass."

"I won't tell if you won't."

She laughed, and he took advantage to flip her over so that he was on his back and she was riding him.

"I like this," she said. "I like being in charge."

"I like letting you be in charge. Just don't expect it all the time."

"I think we're going to have to get a coin that we flip. See who gets to be on top."

"I have a better idea"

"What's that?"

"Right now? I just want you to ride me."

She laughed, but complied, her body rocking

with his, their pleasure rising together. It felt so good to be deep inside her. To have that connection. To be able to watch her face as they went over the edge together.

For a few more moments, he thought about how lucky he was, but then the capacity of rational thought left him. He was only need and lust. His lust. Her need. And a little bit of vice-versa.

As she arched back, her hips rocking as she rode him toward an explosive climax, he slipped his finger between their bodies, so that she was stroking her clit on his hand as she moved. He watched her breasts bounce—and dear God, wasn't *that* hot—and felt how wet she was. How tight. And then, as she spiraled over, he felt her pussy clench around him, the power of her orgasm squeezing him like a vise so that he bucked and moaned and exploded inside her.

Sated, she fell forward, their bodies still connected. He'd deal with the damn condom later. Right now, he just wanted to feel her heat against his skin.

"That was amazing," she murmured as life flowed back into her. "You're amazing."

"I think we've already had this debate," he said, making her laugh.

"I like working out our differences in bed. Maybe next time we should arm wrestle." He laughed, then rolled over on top of her, holding her down. "You might be a bad ass, Ms. Tucker, but I think I could take you."

"Oh yeah? Let's see."

He was about to take her up on that challenge. The idea of having her trapped in his arms was almost too good to pass up. But they were distracted by the ringing of the phone. He reached for it and when he saw that it was Quince, he hit the button for the speaker.

"We've got it," Quince said. "The Serpent gave up the address for Clyde Morgan. We're putting a team together. All we need is you."

"A small team. Emma and I go in. You and Liam are back up outside. Denny in the van on communications and tech."

"That's what we thought you'd say," Quince said. "Be ready in fifteen. We'll come by to get you."

"Where's The Serpent now?"

"His name is Nicol Vartac, and he's been remanded to the SOC. Seagrave is taking him into custody. I imagine he'll be living under the government's hospitality for a very long time."

"And good riddance to him," Tony said.

"We'll be ready when you get here." He ended the call, then frowned at Emma's expression.

"What's wrong?"

"I need to tell you something. I shouldn't, but I don't want any secrets between us."

Now it was his turn to frown. "I'm listening."

"I told you that our missions aligned, remember? When you came to my house after the island. Because your father—well, you know."

"Right. Was that not true?"

"No, no. Completely true. I just kind of left off the part about the rest of the mission lining up, too."

"The Serpent," he said, and she nodded.

"He's been on my radar for years. He was the central figure in a case I worked on in Texas about a billion years ago."

Tony frowned. "Okay. Why didn't you tell me?"

"Nothing to do with him or with you. But—well, you're joining Stark Security. We're together. And I don't want you to find out accidentally."

"I'm still listening."

"I didn't say anything because it's Winston's secret more than mine. We had an overlap on our cases. And The Serpent was right there in the middle of it. Some really bad shit went down and Winston—never mind." She shakes her head. "I'm sorry. I'll share most anything with you, but I can't share someone else's story. I'm sorry."

He shook his head. "Sweetheart, you don't have to be sorry. Believe me when I say I understand about secrets."

"Good. This one's a hard one. Not even Eliza knows."

He laughs. "And yet you told me. I guess you really do love me."

"Guess I do." She rose up and kissed him. "I really do. Now let's go see what the story is with your asshole of a father."

"From what Vartac told us and what we could pull together quickly, it seems that your father went under the knife a lot to change his appearance." Liam shook his head. "Not for the squeamish, that's for damn sure. And apparently the surgeries didn't sit well, because infections have been eating away at him for years."

Quince nodded. "That and plain, old-fashioned ill-health. He's not that old. But from the photos the man looks to be well over ninety. And apparently his days are numbered."

Tony nodded, taking it all in, wondering if it made him a bad person because he really didn't give a shit if his father lived or died. No, correction—he'd rather Clyde Morgan were dead. The world would be that much better.

"So he set this house up under a dozen or so shell accounts, moved in, and hired private nursing care," he guessed.

"Got it in one," Denny said. "Only not nursing care. A nurse. Singular. Your dad's not the most trusting guy."

"Don't call him that."

"Right. Sorry. Morgan's not too trusting. He has one nurse who looks after him. Nine to seven. She'll do overnights if he's in a bad way, but right now, I guess he's chugging along because she left fifteen minutes ago. I had Mario sit on the house while we went and got you two."

"So what's the plan?" Quincy asked. "Are you here to arrest him for the conspiracy to murder your mother and uncle? Vartac confessed. He was a bit looped on chemicals, but I'm sure we could arrange a signed, drug-free confession."

"That's the plan," Tony said, even though of

course it wasn't the plan. Which Quince had to know. Liam, too. They'd all worked together at Deliverance. His friends knew that there was no way Tony was letting that subpar excuse for a human live another day.

As for Denny, he seriously doubted her morals would be tweaked by his intentions, and he knew Emma's wouldn't.

And yet they all still played the game.

He looked at Emma, now dressed in black denim and a black long-sleeve shirt. She looked sexy as hell, and more like a cat burglar than an intelligence officer.

"Ready?"

"Lead the way," she said.

The house had an alarm system, but it was a piece of shit that Denny had hacked through in less than ten minutes. Apparently, Morgan didn't think he was on anyone's radar.

The fact that they were breaking in, though, was further proof that everyone in that van knew he wasn't coming to arrest Morgan. People with the intention to put legitimate cuffs on a criminal didn't break and enter. Plus, they tended to bring someone in law enforcement. Not private security, no matter how prestigious.

At any rate, he was grateful for Denny's

skills, and they were in the house in under three minutes.

"Comms check," he whispered, and got a soft *Roger that,* in response.

He checked his weapon as Emma did the same. Not that he expected a firefight with a decrepit old man, but you never knew. If all went as expected, he'd be using exactly one bullet.

Morgan's bedroom was on the first floor, and they found it more from the stench than the floor plan Denny had worked out. The hall was putrid, stinking of human waste and bodily fluids.

"It's like somebody dumped a truckload of used diapers," Emma commented. "Then sprayed them down with liquefied rotting meat."

"Thanks. If my stomach hadn't already been flipping, it would surely be now."

She didn't answer. Probably so she could go a few more steps without breathing.

The door to Morgan's room was open. He lay like a wraith in a twin-size hospital bed, his frail body barely making a dent under the dingy gray sheet. His face was turned away, and he was looking out a window at a backyard aviary. Maybe wondering if one day he'd have the chance to fly away.

"Father."

Morgan's head turned slowly. As if it took all his strength. His face was lumpy with pustules, his eyes red and runny, his lips cracked and sneering. "You," he rasped. "Why the fuck would anyone think I'd want to see you?"

"I could ask myself the same question about you." He put his hand on his gun as Emma stepped up beside him.

But, dammit, he couldn't bring himself to pull. He knew damn well there'd be no consequences. If anyone could commit a crime and get away with it, he was that man.

But suddenly, he just didn't want to.

Not that he didn't have the stomach for it—he'd still happily dance on his father's grave whenever that celebratory moment came.

No, he was changing his plan because the man was already in hell.

"I just came by to tell you that I'm doing great. Incredible job. Great friends. Smart, beautiful girlfriend. And that's all in spite of you, not because of you. Just so we're clear on that point."

He turned to go, because really, why would he stay? Emma was standing there staring at him, a small grin tugging at her lips.

"He's not worth it," Tony said.

"No. He really isn't."

She started to turn, too, and that's when he heard it. The odd rustling sound. Not like skin against a cotton sheet but something else. Something—

Shit.

He whirled back at the same time Emma did, both with their weapons out, both firing at the old man.

He took Tony's in the chest and Emma's in the head. And the gun Morgan had pulled from beneath the sheet fell from his hand before he got off a single shot.

"He wasn't worth it," Emma repeated. "And now he's no trouble to anyone."

Tony nodded, then took her hand. "Come on, sweetheart. Let's go home."

They stepped through the door together.

And Tony never looked back.

EPILOGUE

I'm pretty sure my bungalow has never had this many people in it. Not that I mind. After all, everyone is here to celebrate my sister and Quincy at their official engagement party.

It's been three weeks since Quince finally proposed, but I'd wanted to be the hostess and Tony wanted to get his things from storage in New York.

So in addition to having more people than the fire code allows, I also have a garage full of boxes. It's wreaking havoc on my obsession with keeping a clean house. And I am absolutely loving it.

"Everyone's having a great time," Tony says, sliding up behind me and wrapping his arms around my waist. "Although I think it's time to cut Quince off."

I'd been looking into the kitchen, wondering if I needed to order another alcohol delivery. Now I turn around to find Quince stumbling onto the hearth, his glass lifted in what I think will be his third—no, fourth—toast to my sister. Everyone turns politely toward him, but nobody's really listening. He's already sung her praises so many times we could all recite them.

To her credit, Eliza doesn't look the least bit embarrassed. And when she turns to beam at me, all I can think is that she looks like a woman in love.

We have that in common now, too.

With Tony's arms around me, I take stock of our lives. Leah is huddled deep in conversation with Cass, and I wonder if maybe there's something there. Damien, Ryan, and Jackson are standing with their wives, Nikki, Jamie, and Sylvia, and since they're laughing I'm assuming it's not business that they're discussing.

I find Mario hunkered down by my stereo system and roll my eyes. But if he wants to suggest upgrades, I won't push him away. And Liam and his girlfriend Xena are on the back patio, watching the rays from the setting sun break through the leaves on the trees.

Mason and Denny are in the kitchen where Mason is making her something non-alcoholic to drink, and from what I can tell, Winston is supervising. As I watch, he pulls out his phone, then frowns as he takes the call.

He moves to the side, then looks up, his brow furrowed as he meets my eyes.

"Trouble," Tony murmurs.

I shake my head. "I don't know." I turn in the circle of his arms to face him, then give him a quick kiss. "I'm going to go check on him."

"I'll mingle. And by that I mean I'll see if I can get Quince off the hearth."

I laugh, then give him one more kiss before heading to Winston. He meets me halfway, then pulls me aside.

"What's going on?" I ask.

"That was Seagrave," he says, his eyes dark and haunted. "Looks like I need to go back to Texas."

The End

A NOTE FROM JK:

I hoped you enjoyed Tony and Emma's story! And I hope you're excited to meet **WINSTON** in *Destroyed With You!*

Be sure to visit www. jkenner.com to subscribe to my newsletter or **Text JKenner to 21000** for text alerts to keep you in the know!

The Stark Security books are set in the world of Stark International, a world that first came to life for me in *Release Me*, Damien Stark and Nikki Fairchild's story. If you haven't read it, I hope you check it out!

And keep reading for a peek at **My Fallen Saint - coming September of 2020!**

**XXOO
JK**

MY FALLEN SAINT
Sneak Peek

"**J**. **Kenner knows how to deliver a tortured alpha that everyone will fall for hard. Saint is exactly the sinner I want in my bed.**"

Laurelin Paige, NYT bestselling author

The wind stings my face and the glare from the afternoon sun obscures my vision as I fly down the long stretch of Sunset Canyon Road at well over a hundred miles per hour.

My heart pounds and my palms are sweaty, but not because of my speed. On the contrary, this is what I need. The rush. The thrill. I crave it like a junkie, and it affects me like a toddler on a sugar high.

Honestly, it's taking every ounce of my willpower not to put my 1965 Shelby Cobra through her paces and kick her powerful engine up even more.

I can't, though. Not today. Not here.

Not when I'm back, and certainly not when my homecoming has roused a swarm of butterflies in my stomach. When every curve in this road brings back memories that have tears clogging my throat and my bowels rumbling with nerves.

Dammit.

I pound down the clutch, then slam my foot onto the brake, shifting into neutral as I simultaneously yank the wheel sharply to the left. The tires squeal in protest as I make a U-turn across the oncoming lane, the car's ass fishtailing before skidding to a stop in the turnout. I'm breathing hard, and honestly, I think Shelby is, too. She's more than a car to me; she's a lifelong best friend, and I don't usually fuck with her like this.

Now, though...

Well, now she's dangerously close to the cliff's edge, her entire passenger side resting parallel to a void that boasts a view of the distant coastline. Not to mention a seriously stunning glimpse of the small downtown below.

I ratchet up the emergency brake as my heartbeat pounds in my throat. And only when I'm certain we won't go skidding down the side of the cliff do I kill Shelby's engine, wipe my sweaty palms on my jeans, and let my body relax.

Well, hello to you, too, Laguna Cortez.

With a sigh, I take off my ball cap, allowing my dark curls to bounce free around my face and graze my shoulders.

"Get a grip, Ellie," I murmur, then suck in a deep breath. Not so much for courage—I'm not afraid of this town—but for fortitude. Because Laguna Cortez beat me down before, and it's going to take all of my strength to walk those streets again.

One more breath, and then I step out of the car. I walk to the edge of the turnout. There's no barrier, and loose dirt and small stones clatter down the hill as I balance on the very edge.

Below me, jagged rocks protrude from the canyon walls. Further down, the harsh angles smooth to gentle slopes with homes of all shapes and sizes nestled among the rocks and scrubby plants. The tiled roofs follow the tightly winding road that leads down to the Arts District. Tucked neatly in the valley formed by a U of hills and canyons, the area opens onto the town's largest beach and draws a steady stream of tourists and locals.

As far as the public is concerned, Laguna Cortez is one of the gems of the Pacific Coast. A laid-back town with just under sixty-thousand people and miles of sandy and rocky beaches.

Most people would give their right arm to live here.

As far as I'm concerned, it's hell.

It's the place where I lost my heart and my virginity. Not to mention everybody close to me. My parents. My uncle.

And Alex.

The boy I'd loved. The man who broke me.

Not a single one of them is here anymore. My family, all dead. And Alex, long gone.

I ran, too, desperate to escape the weight of my losses and the sting of betrayal. I swore to myself that I'd never return.

As far as I was concerned, nothing would get me back.

But now it's ten years later, and here am I again, drawn back down to hell by the ghosts of my past.

Coming September 15, 2020

MY FALLEN SAINT

ABOUT THE AUTHOR

J. Kenner (aka Julie Kenner) is the *New York Times*, *USA Today*, *Publishers Weekly*, *Wall Street Journal* and #1 International bestselling author of over one hundred novels, novellas and short stories in a variety of genres.

JK has been praised by *Publishers Weekly* as an author with a "flair for dialogue and eccentric characterizations" and by *RT Bookclub* for having "cornered the market on sinfully attractive, dominant antiheroes and the women who swoon for them."

In her previous career as an attorney, JK worked as a lawyer in Southern California and Texas. She currently lives in Central Texas, with her husband, two daughters, and two rather spastic cats.

Stay in touch! Text JKenner to 21000 to subscribe to JK's text alerts.

www.jkenner.com

Made in the USA
Columbia, SC
22 May 2022

60762988R00185